A Diary of Dreams

Naomi Sharp

ISBN-13: 978-1505949407
ISBN- 10: 1505949408

DEDICATION

I dedicate this book to all the people who have attended
Spirit of the Phoenix and have had the courage to face
their obstacles and determination to create a better life for
themselves – you truly are inspiring.

Naomi Sharp

CONTENTS

1   Introduction   1

2   Passports at the Ready   Pg 19

3   Map of Dreams   Pg 32

4   Arriving at the Country Fair and Rodeo   Pg 55

5   Around the Stew Pot   Pg 75

6   The Bar   Pg 100

7   Arriving at the BBQ   Pg 122

8   Dreams Becoming Reality   Pg 142

9   Epilogue   Pg 163

1 INTRODUCTION

It was 3am in the morning and Ally still couldn't handle the eeriness of night-time, now her protector was gone everything seemed stiller, spookily stiller. Ally shivered and got goose bumps as the thought crossed her mind. She glanced across at her son Hugh fast asleep in the land of dreams, he looked so peaceful and happy.

It had been six months since Hugh's dad had died, six months, "god where has the time gone" Ally thought. Yet the darkness in her heart still loomed and the pain still shot through her body with every heart beat.

Ally went back to looking through the internet just to pass the time until day break. There was nothing interesting. "When is the pain going to go? When will I stop feeling his absence and start feeling the presence of life? I know his love hasn't gone, it's only transformed" Ally muttered to the night sky.

It was a full moon and there was a pool of moonlight beside her bed. As Ally gazed into the pool of light a thought floated into her head, not quite a thought more a promise she had made – to go on a road trip around America. Yet it never seemed to be the right time; she had planned to do it as a family when Hugh's dad was still alive. "I guess we're still a family it's just now we have a guardian angel instead of a husband or dad" – no sooner had the thought entered her head she'd dismissed it.

Ally rolled over and felt the warmth of the morning sun stroke her face, as she lay there basking in the light, she stretched out her left arm and felt an empty space next to her. A small groan left her lips, no miracles last night, he's still not here. Then she heard the front door close which caused her to screw up into the foetal position – her mom had just arrived. She heard the kettle being switched on and Ally's mom's questions began "where's your mom Hugh?", "upstairs" Hugh replied cheerily, "what is she still doing in bed at this time?" Ally knew it wouldn't be long before her mom would be upstairs pulling the duvet off her.

Yet that still wasn't enough of an incentive to get out of bed. Then she heard her mom's feet stomp up the stairs "Ally! Ally! why aren't you up?" she called, then whoosh the duvet was gone, her warm blanket replaced with cold air "come on Ally, get up!"

exclaimed her mom "time to stop wasting the day" and with that comment she was off down the stairs again. Her mom had taken it upon herself to be Ally's personal alarm clock, not at Ally's recommendation though.

Ally rolled herself out of bed and put on her dressing gown, and made her way to the bathroom. She turned on the tap to run some hot water, she glanced in the mirror and saw the dark rings around her eyes, and another wrinkle to add to the collection. "I look like the walking dead" she said to herself and splashed her face trying to wash away her sadness. When she moved the towel away from her face she looked in the mirror – another wish not granted. The heavy weight of despair sat in her stomach.

"All I have to do is make it through the day" she thought as she ran her hand down the banister as she walked down the staircase. As she entered the kitchen she saw Hugh washing up his breakfast pots, he turned to Ally "morning mom, how did you sleep?" he said merrily. "Ok thanks" Ally replied, jealous of his upbeat happiness. Her mom then entered the kitchen like a whirlwind "so what are you going to do today Ally?" Ally just shrugged her shoulders as she took a sip of tea. Hugh went upstairs to clean his teeth.

Ally's mom took the opportunity to give her daughter another pep talk "what kind of an example are you setting your son" she began "you need to snap out of if for Hugh's sake, for all our sakes. You can't carry on like this, life goes on." Ally had grown accustomed to her mom's morning pep talks on how she was an inadequate mother, Ally just kept drinking her tea, eventually Hugh came back down the stairs. Ally's mom gave one last disapproving look at her daughter. "Come on, Hugh, let's get you off to school before we end up being late" Ally's mom instructed.

Hugh grabbed his rucksack and coat, went over to his mom and gave her a hug "see you later mom, keep searching for your happiness, it'll come back soon." Ally bent down and kissed Hugh on the cheek, she admired his optimism. Then the front door closed and silence descended. Part of her enjoyed the quiet, at least she didn't have to put on a brave face and say everything is ok. She stood in the kitchen contemplating what she should do today. Ally settled on having a shower – that would be her job list for today and then she would hide from life, trying to forget all that has gone on in the past six months, forgetting he is no longer here, continuing to watch the front door waiting for him to come walking in, scoop her up and have a long loving kiss as he apologises for being late.

As the picture of Hugh's dad came into her head she burst into sobs and lowered herself to the kitchen floor, bringing her knees up to her chest. The grieving is never-ending, sadness is now her shadow, there even when she can't see it. Her tear ducts are permanently in use and the pain in her chest hits as she feels each of her heart cells die as she no longer has the one she loves next to her.

Ally mopped up her tears, "come on Ally you can do this" she said sternly to herself "if Hugh can do it, so can I. How did he do it?" she thought. She concluded that he seems happy and has just embraced the change in life – his dad is no longer here. Each night he says to Ally "I know I can't see dad any more but I know each day is filled with his love." Ally began to sob again at the thought of no longer having his arms wrapped around her, making her feel like that was the safest place in the world where any dream could come true.

Ally had accomplished her task for the day even though it took her until 3pm to achieve it, just in time for when Hugh got home from school "Hey Monkey", Ally's nickname for Hugh, "how was your day at school?", "it was ok, nothing exciting" he said while throwing his school bag on the chair, and headed up to his bedroom. Ally watched as he walked by her, she felt so numb, "Monkey what do you want for dinner?", "don't mind" Hugh shouted from the stairs, then he was gone.

As Hugh entered his room, he slumped on his bed. It's not that he doesn't want to spend time with his mom, it's just he doesn't want to feel sad or see his mom so sad. He dreams every night that his mom finds her happiness again. And he knows his happiness annoys his mom. It's not that he doesn't miss his dad, because he does. He realises there will be so many moments in the future when everyone has got their dads with them and he won't have his there, but it's just that he doesn't want his life to disappear and spend all his time regretting all the things he would have liked to have done.

He stared up at the ceiling thinking about what he wants to do when he grows up, the places he wants to see. He smiled as his imagination was ignited with the endless possibilities. Then he thought back to when his dad was alive, his mom made a vision board every year, full of pictures of the places she wanted to go, people she wanted to meet and dreams she wanted to achieve. When dad died she had taken them all down and burnt them in one of her desperate moments crying out "what's the point in dreaming anymore."

Hugh rolled onto his side at the memory of her bad days. He took out a pad and pencil to doodle as his mind wandered over the happenings of the past six months. As the memories started to come flooding back, he stopped them and thought "no, I am not going down the spiral, my mom's wrong, it is right to dream, dreams do come true, she's just forgotten the magic."

He jumped from his bed and began rummaging through his drawers "where are they" he said to himself in desperation. He headed under his bed "surely she didn't get rid of them" he said aloud. He headed over to the bottom of his wardrobe and when he opened the doors he saw the stack of magazines. As he pulled the large pile out they crashed to the floor and heard his mom shout "is everything alright?" "Yes mom" he replied promptly not wanting his mom to come upstairs and see what he was creating.

Hugh began flicking through the pages, tearing out ones that had something that he liked on them and then he threw the used magazine by his door when he felt he had got everything he wanted out of them. The pile of pictures began to grow, he looked at his A4 note pad on his bed, "this dream is way too big for that" he thought. His eyes carried on up to the wall by his bed, "perfect" he whispered.

He went over to his desk and pulled out the sellotape and began to stick the pictures on the wall, places he wanted to go, people he wanted to meet and dreams he wanted to achieve. He couldn't help but bounce with excitement on his bed at the thought of all this coming true. "I'll help mom to remember, remember that love isn't lost, it's just transformed."

Ally was downstairs on the sofa staring out the window watching people pass by, living life with no clue of how precious their life is, or making the most of the time they have with the ones they love instead of wasting it on things that make them feel unhappy. Just as she saw a woman holding her little boy's hand crossing the road she realised how quiet Hugh was and shuffled off the sofa, living seemed such an effort to her as she made her way to his room.

"Is everything ok little man?" she said as she slowly opened his door, not knowing what to expect. As the gap in the door widened, she saw Hugh on his bed with a picture in one hand and the sellotape in the other with the pictures sprawled out in front of him all over his bed. "What are you up to?" she enquired "I'm making a vision wall" Hugh replied, "a vision wall" she asked, shocked, "yes mom, look, these are the places I am going to go to, and over here are the people I am going to meet and over here are all the dreams I am going to achieve."

Ally's eyes scanned the wall; there were definitely a lot of pictures "all in one year?" she asked "no, silly, over the next couple of years." "Instead of a vision board, mom, like you used to do for the year, my vision wall is going to be ongoing. I'll keep adding pictures to it and when I have completed one thing I'll take it down" Hugh instructed. "Oh right" Ally said, still lost in the pictures, "they are incredible dreams" she whispered. As her eyes flowed across the wall, she couldn't help her curiosity. A stir inside her wondered what it would be like to have some of the dreams in her own life.

Ally took in a big breath and stepped back, afraid to get too close to dreaming "I'd best leave you to it" and left his room. Hugh was too engrossed in what he was doing to notice his mom leave. Ally made her way back downstairs and started to cook dinner and make Hugh's packed lunch for the next day. She felt different as she cooked, she couldn't put her finger on it exactly but she just felt different.

The next day was the same routine as her mom arrived like a whirlwind, whipped up Hugh and took him off to school. When she heard the door close and knew the tornado called her mom was well and truly gone, she got dressed and headed downstairs, to make some breakfast. As she sat eating her boiled egg her eyes surveyed the room "when did the house get so dirty" Ally thought?

Ally felt the sudden urge to straighten out her life. "Today things are going to change" she said to the boiled egg as she ate the last bite. She headed to the sink to start the washing up and then cleaned the kitchen to within an inch of its life. She moved to the living room where she switched on the TV and put on the music channel. As she dusted her hips began to sway to the music.

It had been a long time since Ally had danced but the music was infectious as she side-stepped with the hoover. She heard the beep of the washing machine finishing, switched off the hoover and went to hang out the washing and put the next load on. As she was in the garden she looked around and noticed that it also needed some attention but it would have to wait for another day. Ally made her way upstairs to Hugh's room to change his bed sheets.

Ally scooped up the dirty bed sheets from the floor ready to take them downstairs. She looked at Hugh's vision wall and thought of his optimism "I hope he doesn't become too disappointed when these things don't come true" Ally thought as she walked out and closed the door behind her.

Hugh walked through the door and stopped, staring at his mom who was in the living room ironing with a movie on the TV. "Hi Hugh, how was your day?" Ally asked "Good thanks, how was yours?" he said looking around at the clean house, "good" she remarked, still ironing. Hugh put his school bag on the chair and ran upstairs to get changed. As he took off his school clothes and put on his jeans and t-shirt he looked at his vision wall "it's working" he said convincingly.

As he was scanning the places he wanted to visit his eyes fell on a picture of a country fair and rodeo in America. He had part picked it for himself and part for his mom as she used to always talk about America and how they were going to go on a big trip there as a family and have a real adventure. As the thought gathered momentum in his mind a wave of excitement ran from his head all the way down to his feet and he began dancing on the spot as if he was on hot coals. He sprinted out of his room, down the stairs, missing one of the steps and stumbling, but quickly regaining his balance, and carried on running at top speed as he made his way to the living room.

Hugh slid into the living room, surprising Ally, "where's the fire?" she asked staring at Hugh. Hugh positioned himself in front of her and stood on the chair "I have just had the most brilliant idea" he exclaimed as he stretched his arms as wide as he could. Ally looked at him cautiously "you see mom I was just looking at my vision wall, and you know how you used to always say that we were going on a big trip to America, well let's go!" he shouted joyfully.

Ally began to iron again "it's not the right time Hugh" "Mom you're wrong" he said jumping off the chair "it's the perfect time, let's go on the trip, you and me, we'll book the plane tickets, pack our bags and go on an adventure." He couldn't help but bounce up and down with the excitement of all the opportunities that could happen on their adventure.

Ally grabbed another piece of clothing "Hugh it's not the right time" Ally repeated "come on mom it's just

what we need" Hugh pleaded "I said no Hugh, now
drop it" she snapped. Hugh looked up at his mom,
Ally saw the sparkle in his eyes disappear as it was
replaced with tears, Hugh turned and ran up to his
room. Ally stood motionless "my mom was right I am
a terrible mother" she told herself as she felt the self
loathing start to move around her body like poison in
her blood. The feeling that she had avoided all day
then arrived, the familiar feeling of absence of life,
love and, most of all, hope began to descend.

2 PASSPORTS AT THE READY

Jane was sitting on Ally's bed as she watched Ally pulling clothes out of her wardrobe. Jane had called round after receiving a frantic call from Ally the night before, with her repeating over and over "I can't believe I have done it, what was I thinking, why did I think we could do this?" As Jane tried to get a word in when Ally took a breath, which wasn't very often, she found out that Hugh had suggested that they should go on a trip to America and in the middle of the night Ally had brought two plane tickets.

Ever since then she had been finding excuses why not to go and how they couldn't just up and leave, yet she still couldn't bring herself to cancel their reservation. Every time she got close she pictured Hugh's look of utter disappointment when she told him what she had done and she decided she just couldn't let him down or be the one to take the dream away.

They were flying tomorrow; Hugh had already laid his clothes out on the floor, ready to put in his suitcase, and packed his travel bag for the plane. Ally on the other hand was frantically running round the house trying to gather her things.

As Ally tried on another pair of jeans she let out a sigh as they fell from her hips to the floor; she hadn't realised how much weight she had lost over the last six months. "America is supposed to be great for shopping" Jane mentioned trying to calm Ally down "I think it may come to that if I can't find anything to wear" as Ally grabbed a jumper and threw it in the suitcase. "I don't even know what to pack" she exclaimed chucking a summer dress into the case too "I don't know where we are going or what we are going to be doing! I must be crazy!" Ally said frantically.

Hugh walked in and placed some clean clothes from downstairs on the dresser and sat next to Jane on the bed "don't worry mom – we can figure all that out when we get there, we have the plane tickets and have booked a hire car, we will always be able to find somewhere to sleep and eat, worst case scenario is that it doesn't work out and we change our return ticket and come back sooner."

"How can he be so calm about all this?," Ally thought to herself, "my eight year old son is so calm and collected, just embracing the fact that we are going on

a spontaneous adventure and I am freaking out!"
"There is something not quite right about that – I
should be the adult." Ally stopped what she was
doing as she realised that she had been acting like a
child for the last six months. She looked up at where
Jane and Hugh were sat – maybe this trip is really
what they needed.

"Right, what else do I need?" Ally said aloud "Have
you got your tooth brush mom?" "No I haven't" and
Ally disappeared to get her toiletries bag. While Ally
was gone Jane took out an envelope and two diaries
"this is for you and your mom but don't show it to
her until your first night in America." Hugh opened
up the envelope and saw a handful of American
dollars. He closed the envelope and gave Jane a big
hug, "thank you" he said, "make sure your mom
spends it on something wonderful" Jane replied, "I
promise" Hugh said sliding off the bed. "While you
are there you and your mom can both make a diary of
your adventure" Jane instructed. Hugh looked at the
diaries in his hands and looked back at Jane before
making his way into his room, avoiding seeing his
mom.

Ally re-entered with her toiletries bag, "well" Jane said
while standing up "I will see you at five o'clock
tomorrow morning." Ally wasn't listening – she was
fixated with the weighing scales trying to work out if
her bag was too heavy. Jane walked across the room

and gave her a big hug "everything is going to be alright" and with that she left.

Ally put her suitcase at the bottom of her bed and made her way into Hugh's room where Hugh had begun to pack his own suitcase "do you need any help with that Monkey?" "No I can do it mom." Ally leant against the door frame and watched as her son systematically packed his suitcase putting all the trousers together, then tops finishing with pants and socks. "Well I'll go and put the dinner on" Ally said "ok mom" Hugh replied warmly.

Ever since he had found out that his mom had bought the tickets he was doing everything he could to keep the peace so his mom didn't have any reason to cancel the trip. When he had finished packing and closed the suitcase lid, he placed it in front of his wardrobe, where he stood and looked up at his vision wall. He looked at the pictures that were around the American flag, the places he was going to see, the people he was going to meet, and then he saw his dream that he was going to achieve.

He smiled to himself as every cell in his body knew that it would all come true but he couldn't help wonder about his mom, what the trip would bring for her, who she would meet, whether she would find her happiness. Then he heard Ally's voice "dinner's ready." At this Hugh broke away from his vision wall and headed down the stairs.

That night he slept like a log. Ally, on the other hand, was running through every possible scenario that could happen whilst they were out in America and most of them weren't positive ones. They were all 'what if this happens?' and 'what if that happens?', what if, what if, what if! She slid down her bed and pulled the duvet up so only her eyes were visible as her mind kept firing new thoughts at her one after another.

She closed her eyes hoping this would slow her mind and then before she knew it she was asleep. Ally felt a little hand on her shoulder "mom, it's time to get up, it's 4am." She rolled over "it's too early," she had only managed to get an hour's sleep, "Mom we are going to America today." Ally's eyes shot open as her stomach began its own acrobat routine.

She heard Hugh's footsteps as he made his way downstairs, then she heard the tap turn on as he filled the kettle. Ally was still staring out of the window in disbelief that this was really happening. Hugh returned shortly with a steaming hot cup of tea "there you go mom" he said putting it down on her dresser. "I am going to have a shower" Hugh said, Ally just nodded as no words would come out of her mouth.

As she heard Hugh singing in the shower, Ally sat up in bed, lifted the cup of tea to her mouth and took a long sip. Whoever invented tea was a genius as it fits every occasion – celebrations, commiserations, girly nights, tearful nights – a cup of tea is all you need. As her stomach finished its routine Ally placed her feet on the carpet by the side of the bed "it's a new day Ally, full of new beginnings and opportunities" she said to herself, trying to find comfort in what lay ahead of her that day.

"I'm done mom" Hugh shouted across the landing, "ok" Ally replied and made her way to the bathroom. As Ally was finishing getting ready, she heard the front door open and Jane shout "hello anyone home?", "we're just upstairs" Hugh shouted back in response. Then Ally saw Hugh wheel his suitcase down the stairs, thump, thump, thump, as he made his way down.

Ally got her coat, had one last look in the mirror and quickly dismissed her reflection; "it's too early to be worrying about what I look like", she took hold of the handle of the suitcase and made her way down the stairs. As she reached the kitchen Jane stood there with a cup of coffee in her hand "morning sunshine" Jane said. Ally lifted up her eyebrows "morning is three hours away", Jane smirked. "Jane is your car open?" Hugh asked from the living room "yes" she called, then the front door was open and Hugh was pulling his suitcase towards the boot of the car, Ally followed in pursuit to help him lift it in.

When they both got back in the house Jane was just putting her cup in the sink and taking her car keys off the worktop. "Right then, time to hit the road" and made her way out of the front door with Hugh hot on her heels. Ally took one look around the house before closing the door. As she put the key in the lock, not knowing what lay ahead, she knew one thing: that this trip was one giant leap of faith.

Ally opened the passenger car door and got in. As Jane pulled off Hugh started to clap his hands "one team, one dream" he cheered. Jane looked in the rear view mirror and smiled back at Hugh "one team, one dream" she replied. Ally wasn't quite ready to get excited about the trip just yet, it had taken all her strength to walk out the front door and get in the car.

They reached the drop off zone at the airport. Ally hadn't said a word on the drive there, and Hugh was busy telling Jane about his latest creation on the vision wall. As Jane turned off the ignition and made her way to the boot Hugh jumped out and joined her, taking his suitcase out and placing it on the floor. Ally was frozen in her seat as she heard her car door open. "There is no point delaying the inevitable" said Jane as Ally looked up at her. Ally took a deep breath, undid her seat belt and got out.

Jane immediately gave her a big hug "everything is going to be ok and if you have any trouble, get on the next flight back and I'll be here ready to pick you up." Ally couldn't stop a tear leaking out, "thank you for everything" she said. "Oh stop it, it's not goodbye, just see you later" Jane replied chirpily. Ally wiped her tear and made her way to where her suitcase and son were waiting.

They made their way to the departures area and walked through the door. They were then embraced into the throng of people, going this way and that, parents trying to keep their family all together as they were looking at the screens finding out which check-in desk they needed to go to. The airport workers were walking by, talking about the latest gossip in the airport, and the cleaner whistled in the background as he emptied the bins.

Ally felt a warm hand take hold of her own and gave it a squeeze. "Right, yes" Ally said, snapping out of her daze, "desk 11, that's where we need to head to." As Ally and Hugh waited in the queue for check-in Hugh turned to the people behind him where a retired couple stood waiting, "hi I'm Hugh" he said. The woman looked at Hugh "hi I'm Helen and this is Bill" she replied pointing to the man standing next to her. "We're off to America on an adventure" Hugh explained. "Wow that's very exciting, what kind of an adventure?" Helen asked, "a magical one" Hugh said excited. "Where are you going?" he asked "we are heading back home" Helen responded "we have been in the UK to visit friends" she explained.

Ally was oblivious to what was happening as she was too busy watching the people check in one by one.

Hugh smiled at Helen "it's really nice to meet you" and turned back to Ally – he knew this was going to be a great trip. Helen smiled and turned back to her husband Bill. Hugh had an uncanny ability to make friends really easily no matter where he was or who he was speaking to.

As they reached the desk, the check-in lady looked up from her computer screen, "Good morning" the lady said with a glow of happiness in her eyes. Ally began to relax as she placed the suitcases on the conveyer belt and got the passports out of her handbag, "did you pack your own bags?" the check in lady asked "yes we did" Ally replied, leaning on the desk.

Hugh was holding onto Ally's coat examining all that was happening in the airport. The check-in lady handed Ally the boarding passes, "have a great flight" she concluded. Ally took Hugh's hand as they made their way to security. "Right, Monkey, we will get to the departure lounge and have some breakfast", "right you are mom" Hugh said, skipping by her side.

As they sat in the departure lounge tucking into a full English breakfast, Ally was nursing her tea, "first bit over and done with" she thought. She was breaking the day down into little steps and mentally ticking them off one by one as they made their way through the day. Hugh hadn't said much since they had entered security as he saw his mom deep in thought and considered it best to leave her be.

Naomi Sharp

He watched as the different planes took off to their different destinations, "not long now" he thought before him and his mom would be on the plane taking off. His mom could most definitely not back out then, "all that's left to do is to get her on the plane" he thought as he watched another plane take off.

Ally glanced down at her watch, ten minutes until the gate opens. She took one more swig of tea "shall we make our way down to the departure gate?" she asked. Hugh took his coat from the back of the chair, threaded his arms through and hopped off the chair "let's go mom" he replied. Ally stood up, hooked her hand through her handbag handle and they made their way to the departure gate.

When they reached gate 17 Hugh spotted the people he was speaking to at check-in and pulled his mom over to where they were sitting. "Hello again" Helen called out "hi" Hugh replied, "this is my mom" he said pulling his mom closer to him "hi" Ally said holding out her hand, Helen took it and they shook hands "hi" she replied. Her husband Bill looked up from his newspaper and gave her a nod, Helen nudged him "don't be so rude" she said in jest. She turned back to Ally and Hugh "ignore grumpy over there" she said nodding towards her husband.

"Hugh told me you were off on an adventure" Helen asked, Ally smiled wearily, "so it seems" she replied.

Helen saw how Ally didn't have quite the same enthusiasm as Hugh "well good on you, it sounds incredible" she said, trying to lighten the mood. "What made you decide to go on the trip?" Helen asked. Hugh looked at Ally waiting for her response. Ally wondered how many times she was going to have to tell this story as she began to explain the last six months – of Hugh's dad dying and Hugh's vision wall. As Ally reached the present day, Helen was smiling with love "Ah it sounds like the big man upstairs thinks it's time for some healing." Ally looked at her confused "big man upstairs?", "yes" Helen responded enthusiastically, "God, universe, spirit, whatever you want to call it."

Her husband Bill stepped in "oh don't start with that rubbish, you'll scare the woman half to death!" pointing his finger at Ally. Helen sat back in her seat and didn't say another word but looked over to Hugh and winked; Hugh smiled back. Then there was an announcement "gate 17 is now open for boarding." All four of them stood up, picked up their bags and joined the queue. They reached the stand where Ally handed the tickets over "have a great flight" the man said as he handed the tickets back to Ally.

Through into the tunnel they went. As their footsteps echoed Ally's heart began to beat rapidly "I can't do this", "I can't do this" she kept repeating to herself. She could hear Hugh talking to her about something but all she could hear was her rapid heartbeat ringing in her ears. As they reached the plane door they were greeted by a very smiley air hostess "good morning" she said merrily, looking at the tickets Ally had just handed her, "you're just down the aisle on the right." Hugh went ahead and made his way to where the air hostess was pointing. Ally smiled and followed him.

As Hugh reached the seats with the sign 32A 32B 32C he slid in first to make sure he got the window seat. Ally lifted her bag up into the overhead locker and sat in the middle seat watching the plane slowly fill up as people found their seats. "Please no-one sit next to me" Ally said, Hugh looked across at his mom with her eyes scrunched closed and fingers crossed, and went back to looking out of the window.

As the last few people boarded the plane and found their seats, Ally looked at the empty seat next to her and let out a sigh of relief. Hugh turned to his mom "now you're beginning to remember how it works." Ally looked at him dismissing the comment and began to watch the safety demonstration.

The plane jolted into motion as it reversed out and made its way to the runway. The hostess walked down the airplane aisle checking seat belts and that all the lockers were closed before finding her seat. As the plane came to a halt with the long runway ahead of it, Hugh was now intently watching everything that was happening out of the window. Ally took hold of the seat armrests, one in each hand, in a firm grip when the pilot began to rev the engines. In no time at all the plane was moving forward and up into the air, climbing rapidly.

Ally closed her eyes – she hated this bit. The plane began to level out. Ally stopped holding her breath and joined Hugh looking out of the window, watching the clouds pass by. "No going back now" she said, Hugh turned and gave her a kiss, "one team, one dream" he said before turning back to continue looking out of the window.

3 MAP OF DREAMS

Ally and Hugh made their way to the tourist information desk with their suitcases in tow. They reached the desk and a man looked up from his computer "morning mam how can I help?", "hi" Ally replied, breathless from power walking as her adrenaline was at an all-time high. "Two questions", the man just looked at her awaiting the questions, "firstly how do we get to the hire car centre?", "you catch the next bus just outside and that goes to all car rentals – and the next question?" he asked politely. "Do you have a map of the area and any suggestions of places to stay?", "that's three questions" the man said in jest. Ally just looked at him – she was too stressed for jokes or to be corrected. The man quickly continued "here is a map of the city and here is a map of the states, here is a brochure of the local events, and here are some brochures of local places to stay" the man finished.

Ally scooped up the brochures and stuffed them into her handbag, "thank you" she shouted over her shoulder as a bus just pulled up outside. "Have a great day mam" the man replied but he was too late – they had already made their way through the doors and were outside. He took one last look at the two of them before looking back at his computer.

Ally was greeted by a bus driver who was opening up the luggage compartment on the bus. He took Ally's case "where you heading today?" he asked, "the car hire centre" Ally replied. He looked up from the luggage compartment, "I know that but which one?", Ally handed over Hugh's suitcase, "oh right, umm." Ally began rummaging around in her handbag for the paperwork, in the process spilling all the brochures she had received from the tourist information onto the pavement. Hugh bent down and began collecting them, "here it is" Ally said, thrusting the paperwork into the man's face. He took a step back so he could focus on the words, "right you are, that will be the third stop", and with that he made his way onto the bus to the driver's seat.

Ally lowered the paperwork and Hugh looked up at her. It had been a while since he had seen his mom so stressed, maybe this wasn't the time to tell her that he had butterflies in his stomach too. He handed over the brochures. Ally looked at Hugh "thanks Monkey" and placed the brochures back in her handbag. "Shall we?" she said taking his hand trying to sound happy, Hugh smiled back at his mom. She had never been able to hide her true feelings despite appearances.

They got onto the bus and found a seat. The bus jerked into motion as they heard the gears grind into place. They both looked at each other – what had they got themselves into? Hugh watched the world pass by as they navigated their way round the airport, stopping at different car rentals. He looked at the different types of car, "I wonder what type of car mom has hired?" he mused. He thought that it was likely that she had booked a small two-door car to save on money as they passed a small shiny red car.

The bus pulled up at the next car rental centre. The driver turned round in his seat "this is your stop" he said nodding toward Ally and Hugh. They slid out of their seat and made their way down the bus aisle, "thanks" Ally said making her way down the steps. Hugh stopped at the bus driver and held out his hand "thank you bus driver." The bus driver looked shocked, then took his hand and they shook hands, "have a great day" he replied "we will" Hugh said, turning on his heels and making his way down the steps to where his mom was waiting. She had already got their suitcases out, Hugh pulled his suitcase handle up and followed his mom into the car rental reception. He sat on a chair while his mom was at the desk chatting with the lady. Then he heard his mom

laugh and say with delight "yes that would be great!"
Hugh's curiosity stirred as he made his way to his
mom, as he reached her the lady was handing over the
car keys. Ally smiled at the lady "thank you so much",
the lady returned the smile and replied "have a lovely
holiday."

Hugh, none the wiser, looked at his mom puzzled,
why was she so happy suddenly? Ally turned to Hugh
"right little man shall we hit the road?" Hugh took his
mom's hand and they made their way out of the car
rental reception. "What were you talking about with
the car rental lady mom?" Hugh asked, "oh she was
just asking about our trip" Ally replied. That had left
Hugh even more puzzled – what was so funny about
the trip?

They weaved in and out of the mass of cars as Ally
scanned the car park for their car. "There it is!" Ally
said with glee and made a bee-line for a car. As they
approached the car Hugh stopped in his tracks. They
had reached a large pickup. Hugh looked it up and
down, the tyres were nearly as big as him, it was navy
blue and sparkled in the sun from so much polishing.
Ally had already opened the driver's door and was
making her way to the back of the pickup to put her
suitcase in. Hugh shook his head in disbelief and
made his way to the back of the pickup, he couldn't
get any words to come out of his mouth. Ally
chuckled—she had never seen Hugh speechless before.

Hugh made his way round to the side of the pickup, as he reached the door he saw the steering wheel where the passenger normally sits. Ally watched as Hugh was trying to figure things out "they drive on the other side of the road love." Hugh closed the door, and made his way round to the other side where he found no steering wheel, where the driver in England would have sat. He climbed up and into his seat, Ally was already in, and clicked her seat belt in, she put the key in the ignition and the car came to life. Ally melted back into her seat as the purr of the engine soothed her soul. Hugh was sitting staring at his mom "it's time for you to spill the beans mom." Ally came out of her daze and looked at Hugh "well if we are going to be driving miles and miles we are going to do it in style, anyway, it's my treat to myself, I always had a soft spot for pickups, if you run out of tarmac then you hit the dirt road" Ally replied pulling some black shades out of her handbag and slipping them on.

"Right" she said "you're in charge of music and maps, I'll do the driving", "mom, have you ever driven on the other side of the road?" Hugh asked nervously. Ally asked "have you ever read a map?" "no" Hugh replied, "well I guess we are both going to be learning something new today." Hugh couldn't get over how relaxed his mom was. "Ready?" Ally said, partially to herself, partially to Hugh. Hugh shuffled back into the seat and opened up the map and said "ready, let the map of dreams take us to the places and people we are to meet." With that Ally revved the engine for her own enjoyment and the engine roared as they pulled off and were on their way.

As they were making their way down the motorway the airport became a small dot on the horizon. Ally had settled into driving, she surprised herself how quickly she had taken to driving on the other side of the road. Hugh hadn't said much since they had got into the truck, he was too busy absorbing all his surroundings and marvelling at how much bigger the buildings were.

They had decided to tune into the local country radio, one of Ally's favourite songs came on and as she began to sing quietly, Hugh smiled. His mom always used to play this song when dad was alive, dancing around the kitchen. It was one of those moments when he felt his dad's love wrap around him like a big warm blanket. Hugh began to sing along too, as they reached the chorus they both filled their lungs with as much air as they could and sang so loud that it was a sure possibility that people in the next state could hear them. "Life is a highway, I wanna ride it all night long" they belted out as they swayed in their seats. Ally looked across to the car that had come up alongside them and waved to the occupants. She hadn't felt so free in months as they carried on singing with all their might.

They left the city behind and the vast countryside rolled in. "Home" Ally mumbled to herself. Just as that thought crossed her mind the radio DJ announced a country fair and rodeo in town in a week's time with roping, rodeo, barrel racing and lots more. Ally took no notice as she was too busy keeping an eye out for a place to sleep for the night. Hugh, on the other hand, was listening intently and had already got out a pen and was writing the information down on the edge of the map; he found the town that they mentioned and circled it. This must be an omen or a sign he thought as his mind drifted to his vision wall and the picture he had put up there of a country show.

Ally readjusted herself in her seat as her bum had started to go numb. She glanced at the car clock – they had been driving for an hour and to top things off her stomach began to rumble too, the clock confirmed it was lunch time. Ally glanced across to Hugh "do you want to stop off at the next café for some lunch?" Hugh nodded, trying to figure out on the map where they were. Ally looked around for a café and there were just fields to the left and right, but she saw a sign for a turn off. Ally signalled with the indicator and steered the car to the right and headed up the slip road. As they reached the top there was a small café; Ally pulled into the car park, turned off the engine and took her sunglasses off whilst rubbing her eyes.

They stepped out of the truck and made their way into the café. As they found a booth, Ally pulled out the menu and started to look at what they could have. Hugh was fascinated with the different signs and objects hanging on the wall and the juke box in the corner – he had never seen anything like it. "What do you want Monkey?" Ally asked, trying to get Hugh's attention as she saw the waitress approaching. "Hi what can I get you?" the waitress asked, "could I have the chicken burger", Ally replied, "can I have the same please" Hugh said looking back at the walls. "Do you want sodas with that?", "can I have a bottle of water" Ally said, then they both turned to Hugh, Hugh hadn't noticed "and he'll have an orange juice" Ally replied for him.

"What's a soda mom?" Hugh asked, "it's a fizzy drink like the pop we get back home", "so why didn't she just say pop?" Hugh asked bemused. Ally chuckled at the thought of all the things her son had yet to learn as she remembered her first adventure abroad when she was young. The food arrived and Ally took a bite and let out a sigh. She hadn't realized how hungry she was and the taste of the burger was well received by her stomach.

In no time Ally's plate was clean and she watched Hugh taking small bites. Ally slid her hand across the table and stole a chip "hey mom" Hugh said giving her a disapproving look. Ally smiled and turned to admire the truck. She was interrupted as the waitress came over and asked if they wanted dessert. Ally pulled the menu out and glanced over it "can I have some apple pie." She decided she was making up for not eating much for months. Hugh shook his head "no thank you" he replied and they watched the waitress head through a door into the kitchen.

"So any ideas where we are staying tonight?" Ally asked Hugh. Hugh pulled out the map and put his finger to mark where they were now, "well I think we need to head to this place", pointing at a town closest to them. As they were both looking at the map the waitress returned with Ally's dessert. Ally took the apple pie and placed it to the side of the map, Hugh looked up at the waitress "do you know any places where we could stay in this town?" The waitress squinted at the map looking at where Hugh's finger was pointing. "Yes that's where I live. There is a motel just down that street, there is a lovely lady who owns it called Janet." Hugh looked at where the lady was pointing and took out his pen and circled the spot, "thank you" he said smiling up at the waitress "you're welcome, just say Lucy sent you" the waitress added, Hugh nodded and began to fold up the map.

Ally was just trying to fit a large piece of apple pie in her mouth and Hugh stared at her, "hungry mom?" he enquired, Ally blushed. "I've been busted" she thought; she had told Hugh countless times not to put large pieces of food in his mouth and here she was doing the exact same thing. Ally nodded as she tried to stop the stray pieces of apple pie escaping her mouth. Hugh carried on "things are really lining up nicely with perfect timing", Ally swallowed her mouthful, "what do you mean?" Hugh repositioned himself in his seat, "well, you getting the car you love to drive us around on our adventure, turning up at this café where Lucy works who has been able to recommend a place for us to stay and the radio advertising the country fair and rodeo." "What country fair and rodeo?" Ally stepped in, "it was on the radio mom; there is a country fair and rodeo about an hour away", Hugh said, taking the map back out and pointing at a town on the map that he had circled. "Well we'll have to see about that" Ally said uncomfortably "let's just take it one day at a time" as she put the last piece of apple pie in her mouth.

Ally reached over to grab her coat and began to make her way over to the cashier to pay the bill. Hugh lifted the map off the table and walked across the café to his mom. As his mom was putting her purse back in her handbag, "it's an omen mom" Hugh stated. Ally looked at him but before she could say anything Lucy the waitress walked past them balancing dirty pots in her hands, "you should always follow the omens" Hugh said. Ally sighed, she did not have the energy to argue.

"Let's just go to Janet's motel and we'll plan things from there" Ally said dismissively. She made her way out of the café door, Hugh lingered by the café cashier and smiled at Lucy "well at least she didn't say no" he said eagerly. Lucy looked at Hugh "if you let Janet know I sent you, she'll make sure you have a place to stay and are well taken care of."

Hugh came rushing out of the café. Ally was already waiting in the truck; he hopped in and put his seat belt on. "Ready mom" he said cheerily. Ally just glanced across and said nothing. She pulled out of the car park and they made their way towards Janet's motel.

As they drove Ally was following Hugh's instructions and turned right into a street lined with houses. "It should be somewhere along here" Hugh said with his nose pressed against the window. "I'll look this side of the road while you look that side" Hugh instructed Ally. As they drove along slowly looking for Janet's motel they went past different houses with beautiful gardens, some with basket ball hoops above the garage doors, others with immaculate gardens and white picket fences. "There it is!" Ally followed to where Hugh was pointing a few house ahead, there was a sign hanging with 'Motel' written on it.

They pulled into what looked like a driveway and followed the sign for the car park, taking them to the back of the building. Ally drove into a car parking space. Before she had even switched off the engine, Hugh had opened his door and was out of the truck. Ally switched off the ignition and watched Hugh heading towards a sign saying 'Reception'.

Ally grabbed her handbag and leapt out of the truck. This was definitely not the time for Hugh to start going rogue. As Ally reached the door and made her way into the building she spotted Hugh at the reception desk talking to an elderly lady. Ally marched up to him and took hold of his hand, making him jump, "you can't go off like that Hugh" Ally said sternly trying to tame the angry beast growing inside. "This is Janet" Hugh replied, ignoring his mom's anger.

Hugh got his hand free of his mom and put them on the desk, "like I was saying before I was rudely interrupted" Hugh said looking back at his mom "Lucy said to come and see you, can we have a room for two, for a week please?" Janet looked at her screen, "yes of course, we've got room 11 free" she replied in a caring tone. "Perfect" Hugh replied, taking the key being handed to him, "breakfast is between 7am and 8am" Janet said, whilst handing over a pack of information.

Ally took the paperwork and could just about manage a smile. "We can go and get our bags first mom, then head up to the room." Ally made her way outside feeling the angry beast inside her begin to build even more momentum as each thing Hugh said grated on her more and more. They reached the truck, Ally opened the back, Hugh quickly grabbed his suitcase and travel bag and was off to find the room.

Ally slammed the boot shut, to release some of the pressure that was building inside, and made her way across the car park back to the reception. As she entered Janet gave her a warm smile. Ally just walked straight by, down the corridor looking at the numbers along the doors, 3, 5, 7, 11. She turned the handle and pushed the door open. She spotted Hugh with his suitcase on the bed, already unpacking his things. Ally pulled her suitcase onto her bed, and then went to fill the kettle up in the bathroom.

As the kettle was filling she looked up at herself in the mirror "this was such a stupid idea" she mumbled to her reflection. She made her way back into the room and switched the kettle on. Hugh was darting around the room hanging up his clothes, putting his wash bag in the bathroom, as the kettle reached boiling point. Hugh announced to his mom "I'm going to have a look around the place", "hang on before you go." Hugh froze in his tracks – he hadn't made it out the door in time to miss her fury. Ally stood square to him "this has to stop otherwise we are on the next flight home. We're not going to the country fair and rodeo, we are not staying here for a week, there are no such thing as omens, visions walls don't work and

44

things are most definitely not lining up for us" Ally shouted.

Hugh looked at her "so can I go and explore now?" he asked. Ally just turned away "sure"; Hugh exited the room. His mind was whirling with thoughts, "why was his mom so resistant to the change? Why was she resisting things going right? Why did she want to stay unhappy?" he said aloud to himself as the questions kept coming as he walked along the corridor. As he neared reception he saw Janet straightening up the brochures on the stand.

She turned to him "is everything ok?" She stopped re-arranging the brochures and Hugh couldn't keep everything to himself anymore. He burst into tears as he told Janet about his dad, his mom being down, the vision wall, the map of dreams, his mom getting angry with him and all his questions. Janet sat down in the waiting area and motioned for Hugh to come and sit next to her. She pulled out a tissue.

Hugh took it thankfully and then Janet looked at him "your mom has been very brave to bring you on this trip, and has taken a leap of faith. It sounds like she is really trying to find her happiness, but to do that she needs to change her story, but every time she starts to tell a new story guilt just pulls her back to the sad place. She has every right to be angry with life – it has taken away someone who brought her that happiness, and it sounds like she is unsure if she'll ever find that happiness again."

"But I'm still here" Hugh sniffled, "and she is probably just as afraid of losing you too, your mom needs time to heal, to let go, and allow herself to start to create and tell a new chapter, and it sounds like it has already begun. That's a lot of change to handle in a short amount of time and she needs to be able to adjust."

Hugh took a deep breath, "I just need to keep reminding her about the magic, thank you for listening" Hugh said hugging Janet "any time" Janet embraced Hugh.

Hugh made his way back to room 11 and opened the door, as he stepped in he found his mom asleep on the bed with a cup of tea by her bed. He took his duvet and laid it over the top of her and climbed in next to her. Hugging his mom, letting his mind drift over the last 24 hours, he smiled to himself. Everything was going to be ok, they were being taken care of he thought as he drifted off to sleep.

Ally stirred in bed and rubbed her eyes as they adjusted to the light. She reached for her phone – it said 10am. "It can't be" she thought, then she looked down and saw Hugh still fast asleep. She slowly moved out from under the duvet and got out of bed, she replaced the duvet back covering Hugh. Ally headed towards the door, opened it and tried to stop it from creaking, as it closed with a quiet click. Ally walked down the corridor and was greeted at the reception by Janet "morning" she said chirpily. Ally ran her hands through her hair and shuffled her feet "I just want to say about yesterday" but before Ally could say any more Janet stepped in "oh don't worry about it, you have a very special boy." Ally smiled as she thought of Hugh fast asleep in bed "I sure have" she replied. "What would you like for breakfast?" Janet asked "oh it's 10am though" Ally said, Janet raised her eyebrows at Ally. "What have you got?" Ally replied "how about eggs, bacon and mushrooms?" Janet suggested "that's perfect." Ally made her way over to a cluster of small tables in the corner.

As Ally was tucking into her breakfast a sleepy Hugh walked in "morning sunshine" Ally said giving him a big hug and kiss "morning mom" Hugh said croakily. As Hugh got onto the nearest chair Janet appeared with another breakfast "morning Hugh", "Morning Janet". Janet placed the plate in front of him and Hugh tucked in eagerly. Ally took a sip of tea "I thought today we could take a look around the town and pick up some supplies from the supermarket." Hugh nodded as he piled more food into his mouth; Ally smiled, it wasn't the time to correct him especially after she had done the same thing the day before.

Hugh had the directions Janet had given them to get to the supermarket on his knees, as Ally was turning left and then right down the different streets. Hugh couldn't get over how much larger everything was, even the car wash was huge. They saw the sign for the supermarket in the distance and Ally cruised her way to it. Every time she got behind the wheel of the pickup she got a sudden rush of excitement and was well on the way to convincing herself to change cars when they got back to England.

As Ally turned into the supermarket an announcement came on the radio, "this weekend the big country fair and rodeo…", it had got no further as Ally quickly turned the radio off. Hugh looked at her – he knew deep down that they were meant to go to the country fair and rodeo, but how to get his mom to change her mind? Ally kept looking for a car parking space, avoiding eye contact with Hugh so she didn't have to have the conversation about the country fair and rodeo again, even though she could feel his look burning into her heart.

Ally swung the truck and put it into park. "Shall we go and get a few supplies?" Ally said, "sure" Hugh said unenthusiastically, his mind was still on the country fair and rodeo. He came to the conclusion that if he heard the advert for a third time, then no matter what, they were going. Hugh got a trolley and followed his mom into the supermarket, he stopped when he got through the doors. He hadn't seen so much food in one place before – it must have been twice the size of the supermarket back home. Ally was on autopilot starting at the fruit and vegetables and working her way down the aisles.

Hugh started to follow her as she was picking things up and putting them in the trolley. Hugh was engrossed in the different types of foods, some exotic fruits he hadn't seen before. As they turned the corner he saw Ally was already half way down the aisle, Hugh picked up the pace then as the trolley picked up momentum. He pushed himself up so his feet were above the wheels as he free wheeled down the aisle. Just as he was about to reach his mom, he heard a voice call out "Hugh!" Hugh quickly jumped down, his feet landing with a thump on the ground and he spun round. His heart was pounding as he wondered who had seen him. His gaze fell on a couple at the end of the aisle. As he focused on them it dawned on him that it was the couple from the airport line.

He made his way back down the aisle, "hi" he called. Upon reaching them he let go of the trolley handle and put his arms around Helen. "What a coincidence" Helen said, Bill was leaning on the trolley handle and nodded in acknowledgement. "We're here picking some supplies up for the week" Hugh began to explain, "oh right, we are getting some things together for a meal tonight at ours" Helen said. Just then Ally arrived at the trolley and emptied the food she had been carefully balancing in her arms. "Hi" she said looking at Helen, Helen looked back at her husband and turned to Hugh and Ally, "I don't suppose you have anything planned for tonight?" Helen asked. "No nothing" Hugh said eagerly, "well how about you both join us tonight – we are having a few friends over for a meal." "That's very kind of you but we don't wont to intrude" Ally began, "we'd love to" Hugh responded quickly before his mom could pull out. "Awesome, we live…" Helen started to describe how to get to their house, and Hugh pulled out the map from his pocket and a pen, Helen circled where their house was.

Helen said "that's quite some map you got there." Hugh began to explain that it's the map of the people they were to visit and places they were to visit. Helen smiled at Hugh with a knowing look. "We'll see you at 8" Hugh shouted as they went their separate ways.

Hugh and Ally spent the afternoon visiting a few of the places Janet had suggested and then decided to head back to the motel to get ready for the evening meal. As Ally pulled into Helen and Bill's driveway she took a deep breath. Her mind began to wander over how the night's conversation was going to go, how many times she would have to repeat their story. She didn't feel ready for it but Hugh had left her no choice. They couldn't turn down the offer now. She parked the truck and Ally had one last check in the mirror, "you look beautiful mom, you always do" Hugh said. He was wearing a new pair of jeans, shirt and boots that they had picked up at a country store while they were driving around earlier that day. Ally smiled "and don't you look the dashing prince" and kissed his cheek, "mom you'll get lip gloss on me, yuk!" Hugh said in protest.

They got out the car and made their way to the front door. Before they reached the top step the front door was already open and Helen was waiting with arms open wide. Hugh stepped up first and gave her a hug and Ally handed over a bunch of flowers "ah they are lovely, come in, come in." Helen motioned inside. Hugh and Ally stepped in through the front door following Helen to the kitchen where there was already a small group of people gathered. "What would you like to drink?" Bill asked, taking Ally's coat "a glass of wine" she replied, "and you" he said looking down at Hugh "orange juice please".

Hugh went round and introduced himself and Ally to everyone. Ally sure was glad he was here. As Bill handed Ally a glass of wine, they heard a call from the next room "food's ready!" They all filed into the next room and found a seat. Hugh sat in the middle between his mom and Bill. "How was your day?" Bill asked Hugh but before Hugh had chance to answer

Helen called to Bill from the kitchen, "I guess I'm needed" he whispered to Hugh.

Ally had already begun to tell their story to the person sitting next to her and just as she was about to explain how they had ended up in the town Bill came in with bowls of food and a large platter holding a joint of beef. Helen whirled in with the gravy and a few more vegetables. They sat down and bowed their heads to say grace. "Tuck in!" Helen then announced.

The night progressed and Ally was starting to find her rhythm again as she told a few tales of when Hugh was small causing mischief and hiding things. Bill turned to Hugh as he placed his knife and fork down announcing he was officially full, "so are you staying around for the country fair and rodeo?" Hugh stopped with his fork full of food in mid air, "the country fair and rodeo this weekend?" Hugh said, "yes that's right, it's awesome, the biggest event of the year" Bill said. Hugh put his fork down – that was the third time. "It's official, we're going" he thought. Ally had already stopped what she was doing and was looking at Hugh. Hugh turned to Bill "yes we are, we picked up some supplies today and we are going to sleep in the truck or get a tent, I'm not sure which yet, is it for four days?" he asked. "Yes the fourth day is the best as it's the championships" Bill said as his eyes sparkled with excitement. Ally was speechless, had nothing she said the night before sunk in? This had to end once and for all. As she opened her mouth to say something, Hugh jumped in first "mom we are going to the country fair and rodeo, I understand you may be scared, but we are meant to go, the omens are telling us that we need to head to the country fair and rodeo next, please mom, trust me you'll have so much fun, I know you probably can't see that right now, but we have got the rest of the week to rest, sleep and spend time together, so you'll be ready for the country fair and rodeo." The conversations around the table died down as everyone looked at Ally and Hugh. Ally felt the blood begin to rush to her face as she went bright red, she slid her chair back, "excuse me" and went into the kitchen.

Ally leaned over the sink trying to find her breath, trying to keep calm. When she heard someone enter the room she looked up to see Helen standing there. Ally stood up straight and straightened her top, "your son's right" Helen began "it sounds like things are lining up for you both to go to the country fair and rodeo, there must be something you're supposed to do, or someone who you're supposed to meet to help with your journey." Ally looked at Helen, "I'm just trying to get through one day at a time, I thought going away would mean the ache in my heart would disappear, but instead it seems to be getting stronger" Ally said. "Well maybe it's trying to tell you something" Helen replied "in this universe there is only transformation, nothing completely disappears it only transforms, Hugh's dad's love hasn't disappeared, it has transformed, and from what I see your heart is trying to tell you to stop seeing his absence and instead see all the things he has become a part of." Ally didn't know what to say, she knew what Helen was saying was right, but she couldn't bring herself to let go.

Helen made her way across the kitchen and took Ally into her arms "to heal we need to let go of the things that are no longer in the form they once were, to make room to receive the new form they have taken, it's ok, moving on doesn't mean you're forgetting him, it just means you're allowing yourself to still live your life, and move forwards with your story." Ally laid her head on Helen's shoulder and let the tears flow but this time the tears weren't of the pain in her heart, they were of relief.

4 ARRIVING AT THE COUNTRY FAIR AND RODEO

The evening at Bill and Helen's went by in a haze for Ally. Hugh had spent the rest of the evening talking to Bill about fishing and clay pigeon shooting. As Ally and Hugh pulled into Janet's motel and parked the truck neither of them had said a word on the drive home. As they walked across the car park Hugh reached across and took hold of his mom's hand "are you alright mom?" he asked, "yeah I guess" Ally sighed out "I'm just tired" she began, even speaking was an effort. "For the first time I feel free, since your dad that is, I feel I have been carrying a rucksack full of rocks around with me, and tonight I have put it on the ground and walked away. I feel so light, but tired from hauling it around for so long." Hugh didn't say a word, he just let his mom use him as a sounding board. "I can't believe how long I have lived in darkness, and I didn't have to, but I feel lost and unsure what to do with myself now because that's been my purpose for the last six months – to carry that rucksack around, now what do I do?" Ally continued.

"It'll come to you mom" Hugh said as they walked into the reception. Ally squeezed Hugh's hand, maybe things were going the way they should on the trip. They walked past the empty reception desk; Janet must be busy in the back. As they walked down the corridor Ally took out the key and opened the door. They made their way into the room and Ally headed straight to the kettle, "it's definitely time for a cup of tea" Ally thought. Hugh went to the wardrobe and pulled out his travel bag, he placed it on the bed and started to empty the contents. Ally sat on the end of the bed and took off her shoes rubbing her feet, she wasn't used to wearing heels again.

Hugh made his way across to where his mom was and sat down next to her. Ally looked across to Hugh and her gaze fell on two books Hugh had in his lap. "What are those?" Ally asked. Hugh held the books tighter "they are a gift from Jane, she gave them to me before we left and said I should give one to you on our first night which didn't feel right at the time but tonight I think you should have it." Hugh placed one of the books in Ally's lap, Ally opened it up and saw blank diary pages. Ally looked across at Hugh,

Hugh looked at his mom "I think it's time to start to tell your new story mom, I have one to." Hugh opened up his diary and turned to the page with today's date on, Ally noticed how his pages already had writing on. "I started mine when we landed, my new story, the different people we have met, how they have helped us and the places we have been to."

Ally took a deep breath; she was taken aback by what both Jane and Hugh had done. Hugh then pulled out an envelope from the front of his diary, "she also gave us this, to spend on something, I would like to spend mine on buying two tickets for the country fair and rodeo." Ally looked in the envelope and counted the dollars, she looked at Hugh and handed the envelope back to him. Hugh jumped off the bed and started to make his mom a cup of tea; Ally stared down at the diary and flicked through to today's date, and stared some more at the blank page, "a new story…" she thought.

Hugh then handed her a cup of tea and sat back down next to her. Ally closed the diary and held the cup in both hands, feeling the warmth radiate from her hands, up her arms and around the rest of her body. Ally took a sip and looked straight ahead. "Ok if that is what you want to spend your money on, that's your choice and we'll go to this country fair and rodeo." Hugh leapt up and hugged his mom, spilling tea in the process. "Mom you're the best, you won't regret this." Ally brushed tea off her trousers, "a new story, hey, let's make sure it's a good one" she smiled. "Ok Monkey, time for bed", Hugh was too excited to go to bed but went to put his pyjamas on and cleaned his teeth. He was happy to do whatever his mom asked, especially after she had finally agreed they could go.

Hugh climbed into bed and pulled the duvet up so it sat just under his chin. Ally put her cup of tea down and went across to give him a kiss "sweet dreams" and turned off the light. Ally sat back down on the end of the bed and picked her cup up, sitting in the dark drinking her tea, she didn't know what to think or feel any more. Then out of the darkness she heard Hugh's snoring, Ally took her tea into the bathroom and started to run herself a bath. As the water began to fill the tub she went back into the bedroom, collected her pyjamas, picked up the diary and got a pen from her handbag.

As she stepped into the bath she let out a sigh of relief. She ached not from any physical work but from the tension she had held in her body for the last six months. As she felt her muscles relax one by one, she let her mind focus solely on her breathing. One of the most precious things in life, something we take for granted, she thought, but without it, there would be no life to live. Her mind watched as she breathed in and then out, feeling her chest raise up and down, her mind began to quieten and a peaceful feeling filled her body.

Ally opened her eyes and then closed them again quickly as the bathroom light was too bright. Ally tried again and was able to keep her eyes open long enough for them to adjust. She picked up the towel that was on the side, dried her hands and reached for the diary. She turned to today's date; picking up the pen she began to write:

Dear Diary,

Today is the day that I choose to start telling my new story. For the first time I feel free from myself, from my experiences, and most of all from my thoughts. I choose to think about my future being bright, happy and full of love.

I know each day won't be perfect and at the moment I don't know if I can feel the happiness I once did. I may never feel it again but I am going to dream and start to find the magic of life again. Like Helen said, it hasn't disappeared, it has transformed, I just need to find what it has transformed into.

Most of all I want to say thank you to life, for giving me such a special boy, if life hadn't happened like it did I wouldn't have had the chance to hear the wisdom Hugh has to share with us all, thank you for giving me the courage to go on this trip, and bring the people and places into my life with perfect timing.

I am not bouncing round the room with happiness yet, but I do feel relief and that's a start I suppose. That's where my story begins, I feel relief that I no longer have to carry the heavy burdens that I have created with my own imagination.

Love always

Ally

Ally placed the diary down, and just lay in the warm water, embracing the peacefulness that was filling each of her cells. As the bath began to cool down and Ally looked at her fingers that had become wrinkled, she climbed out the bath. Her limbs felt heavy; she dabbed off most of the water and put her pyjamas on. She picked the diary up and opened the door. As she turned off the bathroom light, the darkness returned, but this time she didn't feel the same eeriness she usually felt. Ally felt her way through the dark room to the side of her bed where she pulled back her duvet, placing the diary on the bed side table and got into bed, pulling the duvet up around her chin, she closed her eyes and drifted into the land of dreams.

As the days passed before the weekend of the country fair and rodeo, Bill took Hugh fishing and Helen and Ally went shopping for some retail therapy. Ally and Hugh decided to spend their evenings watching movies or talking with Janet. They had arranged that they would follow Bill and Helen to the country fair and rodeo and set up camp near them. The day before the country fair and rodeo they got sleeping bags, pillows, cushions and blankets as Hugh decided that they were going to change the back of the pickup into a den. Ally spoke with Helen who said they could use their mobile home for cooking and showers.

The night before they set off for the country fair and rodeo, Ally was in the bath, thinking back over the last few days. She had enjoyed the week so much, and felt more refreshed than she could ever have imagined. She looked down at her bright red toe nails and her French manicured finger nails. She hadn't had such a girly week in years. As Hugh lay on his bed he pulled out his diary.

Dear Dan the Diary,

We have got all the things we need for tomorrow and I have packed my suitcase. I knew the vision wall would come true, I love the magic of life. Mom is starting to believe in life again, she still has her sad days but I know she feels better. I know what I want to happen when we are at the country fair and rodeo. I am going to learn how to rope, and make new friends, and mom is going to feel love again. I am so excited. Bill has been telling me all about the rides, team roping, barrel racing, stalls and fair rides. It's going to be incredible. Bill and Helen are going to be staying with us and Bill promised he would take me to see the different things which he has been to every year since forever. Life is magical Dan the Diary! And when I grow up I am never going to forget the magic.

Hugh

The morning sunlight shone through a gap in the curtains. Hugh turned over in his bed, as the light rolled onto his face he felt the warmth of the sunshine. Suddenly his eyes shot open "it's today!" he exclaimed. He flung back the duvet with excitement, "mom, mom, get up, it's the fair!!" he yelled as he bounced around the room with excitement. Ally stirred under the duvet "another five minutes" she sleepily mumbled. "Come on mom we're going to the country fair and rodeo today, there's no time to sleep, GET UP!"

Ally peeled back her duvet as Hugh pulled back the curtains illuminating the room with sunshine. Ally sat up in bed. As her body slowly woke up she watched Hugh dart into the bathroom and turn on the shower. Ally got out of bed and heard Hugh begin to sing in the shower, "Life is a highway, I wanna ride it all night long, if you're going my way, I wanna drive it all night long."

Ally couldn't help but smile to herself as she let Hugh's happiness wash over her. She walked across the room and put the kettle on, then put her suitcase on the bed ready to pack the last few things. As she was just taking her first sip of tea Hugh came out of the bathroom all ready and dressed with his toilet bag under his arm. He threw it on the bed and went over to the wardrobe. He took out his travel bag and suitcase and put them on the bed too, and packed.

Ally meandered across the room to have a shower, in
no particular rush. As she climbed in to take a shower
she saw a note being pushed under the door and then
heard the door of their room close. Ally stepped out
the shower and picked up the note "gone for
breakfast, love you, Hugh." Ally placed the note next
to the sink and got back in the shower.

Hugh skipped down the corridor to where Janet was
laying the breakfast table, "morning" Hugh said
whilst giving Janet a big hug, "morning sunshine"
Janet replied giving him a squeeze in return. "Are you
ready for the big day?" "you bet ya" Hugh replied not
being able to keep still while sitting at the table as he
had too much excitement pumping through his
blood. "You had better have a full English to set you
up for the day" Janet said, making her way to the
kitchen.

Hugh turned to look out the window. He wasn't
looking at anything in particular but as he stared, his
imagination fired up and he saw in his mind the fair,
setting up where they were going to sleep, and seeing
everything there was to see with Bill, Helen and mom.
He ran through the whole day like he was watching a
movie of his future, his grin grew with anticipation.

"Hello Monkey" he turned around to see his mom
taking a seat at the table, "morning mom." Janet
appeared with two full English breakfasts. "This
should keep you going for a while" placing the plates

down. Hugh's breakfast didn't last long, he guzzled it up in minutes. Janet appeared with her morning coffee, "have you got everything you need?" she asked, "yes thank you, thank you so much for everything" Ally replied. "You're welcome, it's great to see you so full of life, you're definitely not the same women who walked through that door a week ago" Janet chuckled. "No I guess not" Ally smiled thinking back to what she must have looked like a week ago – angry, tired and stressed.

"They're here!" Hugh said jumping off his seat and running out of the reception door across the car park to where Bill and Helen were just parking up their motor home. Hugh opened up the driver's door, "hi" he said cheerily, "morning son" Bill replied taking off his seat belt and stepping out of the motor home. "Are you all ready?" he asked "nearly, we just need to pack up the pickup" Hugh said. With that he was gone, running back across to the reception. He shot through the door and was off down the corridor to get his bags.

Bill and Helen walked into the reception where they were greeted by Janet and Ally. Janet stood up "do you want a coffee?" she asked Bill and Helen, "that'll be great" Helen said. Ally got up and gave them both a hug, "how are you doing?" Helen asked. "Surprisingly good" Ally said, shocked at herself. Hugh appeared wearing his coat, carrying his travel bag and pulling his suitcase along. Ally looked towards Bill and Helen, "I'd best finish off packing before he leaves without me." They all laughed as they watched Hugh power walk across the car park on a mission to the pickup.

When Ally returned after doing one final check of the room, Bill, Helen, Janet and Hugh were all sat around the table, telling stories about the previous fairs. Hugh was silently engrossed in every word they said. Ally left them to it and went to load up the truck with her things. As she entered the reception, "ready!" Ally announced. They all stopped talking and began to stand up. Ally walked across to hug Janet "thank you again, I couldn't have done it without you", "glad you got the healing you needed, any time you need a rest or a break, the doors are always open" Janet said. Then Hugh stepped up "thank you" he said "you're welcome super star, you keep spreading that happiness, and following your map" Janet said humbly. "I will" Hugh said winking back.

With that they made their way out to the car park. Bill and Helen got into the motor home and Hugh climbed into the truck. Ally had one last check in the back to make sure they had got everything they needed and got in, she took her shades out and put them on. Hugh turned the radio on and pulled out his map. They pulled off, following close behind Bill and Helen's motor home, waving to Janet who was standing in the reception doorway, and they hit the highway.

Ally checked the clock. They had been driving for two hours and she shuffled in her seat trying to get rid of her numb bum. They started to see the signs for the country fair and rodeo. Hugh had been talking non-stop the whole way there; he couldn't contain his excitement any more. He had been telling Ally of the stories he had heard over breakfast, the different stalls that were going to be there and the competitions he was going to watch. Hugh had planned each day, knowing what arena and at what time he needed to be there to watch the competitions.

Ally just embraced being Hugh's sounding board this time. Hugh then went silent as they had reached the entrance. Bill and Helen slowed down to be greeted by a man checking the tickets and giving directions to the car park. Ally watched Bill and Helen pull forward and Ally moved the truck up to where the man was standing and wound down her window. "Morning mam" the man said "tickets please." Ally reached into her handbag and pulled out the tickets, handing them to him, the man looked at them and then handed them back, "just follow the motor home in front" and with that he moved onto the car behind.

Ally flashed Bill indicating they were ready, and Bill started to move forward. Hugh's nose was pressed up against the window; he'd never seen so many cars, trucks, trailers and motor homes. "Mom" he began "hold on Monkey, let me just park up first, I don't want to lose Bill and Helen", as her eyes were glued to the motor home in front. Bill indicated left for Ally to turn and park next to them. Ally turned in and switched the ignition off. She let out a huge sigh; she had been holding her breath ever since they had come through the entrance.

"Yes, Monkey, what is it?" she said turning to Hugh, "it doesn't matter" he replied as his attention was hooked on his surroundings. Hugh reached for the door handle, "hang on", Ally said "ground rules, you always have your phone switched on, if you get lost you come straight back to the truck, and you always let one of us know where you are going." Hugh leant across and kissed Ally on the cheek, "yes mom", and with that he got out of the truck.

Ally looked around at all the people wearing cowboy hats with horses and cows, she had never seen anything like it, it was so much better than she had imagined. "Right then, a new story" and then the butterflies began in her stomach as her mind began to fill with doubts. "What if I'm not ready for a new story?" It had only been a week, "what if something goes wrong and I go straight back to the way I was?" she thought. Bill's voice broke through her thoughts "Ally!" he shouted. Ally opened the door and got out, she walked around the back of the pickup to see the three of them stood together. "If there are any problems we meet back here" Bill began "we all have each other's phone numbers just in case, me and Hugh are going to go and check where things are." He pulled Hugh closer into his side. "Good, then there's less chance for you to get under my feet while we set up" Helen said playfully.

With that Hugh and Bill disappeared into the sea of vehicles. Helen went into the motor home and then appeared at the door with a chair. Ally reached up and placed it outside on the ground; Helen kept passing more chairs out and then a table. Ally stuck her head through the door, "anything else?" she asked, "no, that's it for now" Helen replied. She was rummaging through the cupboards, mumbling to herself "I'm sure I packed it, I hope that grump hasn't taken it out, there you are" she said, happily pulling out a bottle of champagne. Ally smiled "time for a sneaky one?" Helen suggested. "Most definitely" Ally replied, heading to the back of the pickup and grabbing some strawberries she had bought the day before.

They took a seat at the table outside. Helen poured them each a glass. "Cheers, here's to dreams coming true", "to dreams coming true" Ally replied. She still couldn't quite believe she was really there. They settled into the chairs and began to chat. While Helen was pouring them both another glass, Bill and Hugh reappeared. "I see the unpacking is going well" Bill said jokingly to Helen. He got a glass for himself and an orange juice for Hugh. As they all sat round the table, Hugh lifted up his glass "here's to the magic of life"…"the magic of life" they all said in unison with a clink of their glasses.

"We found all the arenas and there is a bar that does food over there" Hugh said pointing behind him. "Then the stalls are over there" pointing over his other shoulder. "And there is a stage over that way, they have live music every night" Hugh said not knowing what to do first. "Sounds good to me, maybe we could check that out one night" Ally said as she gazed up at the blue sky and let the warm sunshine wash over her.

"Mom can we go and watch the roping at 4 o'clock?" Hugh asked looking intently in the direction of the arenas, trying to make out what was going on. "Yes, sure" Ally said as the champagne was dissolving away her butterflies. "Mom that would mean now, it's nearly 4"; Ally looked at her watch, where had the time gone? She shuffled in her chair, sat up and placed her glass on the table. "Ok, Monkey, let me just grab my handbag." She began to stand up and then sat immediately back down. Bill and Helen began to laugh, "lost your sea legs?" Bill chuckled. Ally took a deep breath and tried again, this time she remained standing and looked across to Helen.

"You're a bad influence" she said laughing. "Just living the good life" Helen replied, lifting her glass.

Ally opened the pickup door and got her handbag, putting it over her shoulder; she shut the door and pressed the lock button. Hugh came round to where Ally was standing and took her hand, "don't worry mom I know the way" he said pulling out a map of the fair. Ally looked down and noticed he had circled the arenas with the competitions he wanted to see, the car park where they had set up camp, and a bar, not too far from the car. "At least one of us does" Ally said concentrating hard to walk in a straight line. As they made it out of the sea of cars, the champagne started to wear off and her nerves returned. In front of them all they could see were hundreds of people – some walking and others on horseback.

"This way mom" Hugh said, pulling at Ally's hand. They weaved in and out of the throng of people. Reaching the arena side, Hugh climbed up to get a better view. They heard the announcement of the first roping team as they entered the starting box and backed the horses into the corner, ropes poised. A nod was given and off the cow went with the cowboys in hot pursuit, one swing of the loop, two swings, then the loop flew through the air, as the cowboy dallied up and they were done, in seconds. "Did you see that?" Hugh said, not taking his eyes off the arena as the next team got ready. "I sure did" Ally said, it was so much better live.

They spent the rest of the afternoon watching team after team rope the cows. As the last team went Hugh climbed down and began retelling everything that he had seen, as Ally walked alongside. "I'm going to get a rope", he began, "can we head to the shop stalls, mom?", "yes, sure" Ally said. She had never felt so full of life. Maybe Hugh had been right – this trip to the fair was going to be alright after all. She smiled to herself "well he's been right about everything else so far", she thought.

As they made their way through different shop stalls full of saddles, bridles, clothes and food they came to a stall that was selling ropes. Hugh dived in, "this way mom" he shouted as he saw his mom scanning the crowd for him. Ally scooted across and joined him. He began picking up a rope, Ally took hold of his arm "you can't go grabbing stuff, you need to ask first" as she saw an elderly gentleman make his way across. "Do you know how to rope son?" he said in a deep voice. "Yeah, a little" Hugh said, starting to build a loop, "why don't you try and rope the roping dummy?" Hugh looked to where the man was pointing, and made his way across, he tried to get the roping dummy's head, but fell short.

"Why don't you try this rope?" the man said, handing him a bright green one. As Hugh kept trying to get the dummy another family entered with a young boy about the same age as Hugh. Ally looked across to what looked like the young boy's parents, smiled and nodded in acknowledgement. The young boy had taken a rope and had joined Hugh at the roping dummy. Ally watched as the young boy roped the dummy straight away. Hugh tried again and missed. "You're not opening your left hand to let the coils out" the young boy said. Hugh looked at his left hand where his knuckles were white from holding the rope so tight. He loosened his grip and tried again. This time the rope travelled through the air and wrapped itself around the roping dummy's horns. "Yeah!" Hugh shouted, looking back at Ally, "well done Hugh" Ally replied.

"My name is Aden" the young boy said looking at Hugh, "I'm Hugh." Together they practised roping, sharing tips and tricks. Ally watched as Hugh started to get it every time. "Hi" Ally turned around "I'm Sally and this is John, we're Aden's parents", "hi, I'm Ally, pleased to meet you." "Are you staying for the whole thing?" Sally asked. "Yes, we met a couple in a town a few hours away and we are staying next to their motor home, it's a long story" Ally said thinking back to how bizarrely everything had worked out over the last week. They had met Lucy who had led them to Janet, they had met Bill and Helen at the airport who had brought them to the country fair and rodeo. "Lots of coincidences, that's for sure" Ally thought.

"Sounds like you've had some trip" Sally said. "You could say that" Ally laughed. Sally began to explain where they had come from and how the country fair and rodeo was their annual holiday. Ally responded with the story of how the trip came about and what had happened over the last week. Sally and Ally hit it off like they had been friends for years. "What are you doing for dinner tonight?" Ally asked. "We are probably going to the bar to grab something there", "why don't you guys come to the motor home – I'm cooking a stew and there will be enough to feed an army" Ally said.

"Anything to have a night off cooking" Sally said, nudging Ally in jest. "Brilliant" Ally said joyfully, it had been a while since she had cooked for others but she found Sally and John so easy to get on with. "Monkey" Ally said trying to interrupt Aden and Hugh who were in deep discussion about who was going to be the header and who was going to be the healer. "Hugh!" Ally shouted louder, Hugh looked at his mom, "time to go – Sally, John and Aden are going to have dinner with us tonight, which I really need to start preparing" Ally said impatiently. "Awesome!" Hugh responded.

Ally turned to where Sally and John were stood "head over in an hour", "sure" Sally replied "we'll provide the wine." Ally took the rope out of Hugh's hand, with Hugh not noticing, and walked across to the man at the stall. She pulled out the envelope that Jane had given her and Hugh. "I'd like this please" she said, handing him the rope. "Do you want a bag?" he asked, "no thanks" Ally said, exchanging the rope with dollars. She walked back over to Hugh and placed the rope in his hands, "in exchange for one country fair and rodeo ticket, take care of it" she said. Hugh looked at his mom in disbelief then wrapped his arms around her "you're the best mom ever!"

"See you later" Hugh shouted to Aden over his shoulder as Ally was pushing him out the door. Ally turned to Sally and John "see you guys in an hour" and with that Ally and Hugh disappeared into the crowds.

5 AROUND THE STEW POT

Ally and Hugh arrived back at the motor home where Bill and Helen were inside setting up the last few things. Hugh rushed in "we're back!" Bill stopped what he was doing and sat down, "so what did you see?" he asked. Hugh began an account of what they had watched at the team roping competition, practising with and buying the rope, and meeting John, Sally and Aden. Ally turned to Helen, "I hope you don't mind but I have invited a couple more people to dinner", "the more the merrier" Helen said pulling out the stew pot.

Ally made her way over to the pickup and began unpacking the vegetables that she had brought from the supermarket, putting them on the table outside. Helen appeared with the chopping board, knife and peeler. "What's first?" she asked "nothing, you relax, you're having a night off from cooking" Ally said smiling. "I could get used to this" Helen said sitting on a chair opposite Ally. "So how was it?" Helen asked. "Incredible" Ally beamed "the way the horses behaved and the accuracy of the roping, there definitely isn't anything quite like it back home, the vibe around the arena was electrifying."

"Spot any good looking ones?" Helen probed, "there was this one, it was a stunning bay mare, with a white blaze and she had blonde streaks through her mane and tail, she was on the money" Ally described. "No, not horses, men!" Helen said eagerly. "Ha, no I can't say I even noticed" Ally said, Helen raised her eyebrows not convinced. "Hugh, can you come and help me please?" Ally called. Hugh appeared at the door "can you wash your hands and then you're in charge of peeling the potatoes", "sure mom" as he disappeared back into the motor home.

Bill followed Hugh outside. As Hugh began to peel the potatoes he carried on telling Bill his story, telling him about the roping dummy and getting it every time with his new rope. Ally zoned out, Helen's questions had stirred something inside of her and it didn't feel comfortable. The more she thought about it the angrier she felt inside, her thoughts began to take hold, "is coming to the fair not enough? Now I have to start looking for a new man, what if I want to be a widow for the rest of my life? What if I never want to kiss another man again? They only go and leave you alone to live life in sorrow" she thought to herself.

Her thoughts began to gather more momentum as she started to chop the vegetables more vigorously. A carrot flew across the table. Everyone stopped what they were doing and looked at Ally. "Everything alright?" Bill asked, placing the runaway carrot back in the stew pot. "Yes of course it is, why wouldn't it be?" Ally snapped back. With that she disappeared into the motor home. Everyone looked at each other trying to figure out what had just happened. Bill stood up and followed Ally into the motor home.

Ally was trying to light the gas stove but was struggling to find the matches as she opened the cupboard and then slammed the door closed again in frustration. Bill opened the drawer to the side of the cooker and took out the matches. "So are you going to tell me what's wrong or am I going to have to figure it out whilst I am replacing the hinges on the cupboard doors?" Ally lit a match and turned on the gas. As the stove came to life she placed a pan of water on it. "Sorry I didn't mean to damage your cupboards" she mumbled, avoiding eye contact. She didn't want Bill to see her tears beginning to build. "Don't worry, I made them, it would take more than a slam to break them" Bill said coming up and wrapping his arms around Ally. "So are you going to tell me what's wrong?"

Ally took a deep breath "I just don't know if I am ready to love again, I don't know if I'll ever be ready to love another man again, sometimes I feel so strong, and other times I feel like a leaf could knock me over. I just don't want to feel sad any more, I want to start enjoying life again, but at the same time I don't want to be pressured into doing anything, maybe what I have right now is as good as it's going to get, and I'm ok with that." Ally had to stop as she couldn't get any more words out as the tears flowed.

"No-one is asking you to fall in love again, get married and live happily ever after. You're stronger than you know and courageous, but there is no point spending the rest of your life using all your energy dodging opportunities of happiness and love just because you're afraid of what it may develop into" Bill continued. "Don't go looking for love, but at the same time don't go avoiding love either. You deserve a life of happiness and love. At the end of the day all you'll have when you're six feet under is your story, so make sure it's a good one, not one of regrets but one of adventure, joy, fun, laughter and love with friends and family."

Ally lifted her head off Bill's chest. "Since when did you become a wise old sage?", "hey you, less of the old, I've still got many miles left and many hours of tormenting Helen too." They both laughed at the thought of Bill causing mischief and Helen pretending to be mad even though she always ended up laughing.

"Thanks, I needed that" Ally said taking a step back and wiping away the tears. Hugh appeared at the doorway, holding the chopping board with potatoes on, "here you go mom", "thanks Hugh, I will put those on now, the stew will be ready in 30 minutes." Hugh handed the chopping board over to Ally, "can I go and rope now?" Hugh asked shyly. "Of course you can" Ally smiled, trying to pretend everything was alright. "Wait for me little man, I'm sure I have an old rope lying around somewhere" Bill said rummaging in a cupboard. Ally looked at Bill "don't you go injuring yourself", "as if, I'm 25 up here" Bill said, pointing to his head "and that's all that matters!"

Hugh and Bill headed out of the motor home and began looking for something to rope. Ally had one last check of the dinner, everything was on track, she looked at the clock – it wouldn't be long before Sally, John and Aden arrived. She collected the knives and forks and then headed outside to lay the table. As she began setting the places Helen got up. "I'll open another bottle" she said, placing her hand on Ally's shoulder as she passed.

Just as Ally finished setting the last place she heard mumbles in the darkness. Sally, John and Aden came into sight; Aden darted straight past the table to where Bill and Hugh were roping, and joined in. "Hey, how you doing?" Ally asked, giving Sally a hug "we've come with goodies" Sally said lifting up two bottles of wine. "Perfect" Ally said as she moved across to give John a hug. She took the beers out of John's hands "I'll put these in the fridge, do you want one now?" she asked him "yes" he replied. "Make that two" a voice behind them called. Ally turned to see Bill leaving the boys to roping the bale of hay they had found. Bill made his way across to where everyone was standing. "Hi I'm Bill" as he shook Sally and John's hands, he then turned to Helen to shake her hand too. "Ha after 30 years of marriage I think we're past the introductions" she said as she placed a beer in his hand. He leant across and gave her a kiss.

"I'll just go and check on dinner" Ally said "do you need a hand?" Sally asked. "No I have two thanks" Ally said, jokily waving her hands in the air as they all laughed and sat down at the table. Ally returned with the pan full of potatoes and put it in the centre of the table and went back inside to collect the stew. "Dinner you two" Ally called across to Hugh and Aden, as she placed the stew on the table and took off the lid.

The aroma of stew filled the air, "the stew smells good mom" Hugh said, sitting down at the table. "Let's hope it tastes good too" Ally replied as she began serving everyone. As she finished putting stew on her plate, she sat down and they lowered their heads to say grace. "Tuck in" Hugh announced filling his mouth with potatoes.

Laughter filled the air as the wine flowed and the stew disappeared. Bill had spent the evening teasing Helen and Helen was trying to avoid the temptation to throw potatoes at the grump. "Right, Monkey, your turn to wash up" Ally said leaning back in her chair as she surveyed all the empty plates around the table and the empty stew pot. "You too Aden" Sally said. Hugh began collecting everyone's plates and taking them inside; Aden followed carrying the stew pot and potato pan into the motor home.

Bill lifted the bottle of wine up to the light. "I'd best get another one of these then" he said getting up, reaching inside the door and pulling out a full bottle of red wine. He began filling up the empty glasses. "Do you come here every year?" Helen asked Sally. Sally began to explain that they take their annual holiday here as it was where she and John first met. "I seduced her with a good looking herd of cows" John said proudly, taking a sip of his wine. "I just felt sorry for the poor buggers having to put up with him every day" Sally corrected, winking at him.

"How long have you been together?" Ally asked. "15 years now I think" Sally said, working her way back through the years, "actually it's 16 years this autumn" John said looking at his wife in disbelief that she couldn't remember how many years they had been together. "What?" Sally shrugged chuckling at her husband. "How did you two meet" Sally said looking at Bill and Helen, "the local dance", Helen began "he was quite good on his feet when he was younger", "hey I'm still an incredible dancer don't you know" Bill proclaimed "age has nothing to do with it" he continued.

"What about you Ally?" Sally asked "how did you meet Hugh's dad?" "It is no fairy tale – I had broken down at the side of the road and he stopped to help. He towed my car back home for me and then I asked him if he would like a cup of tea, and that was it, he never left", Ally said looking up at the stars, reminiscing about that fateful day. "Do you think you'll have another man?" Sally asked. Ally took a gulp of wine and carried on looking at the stars, she felt Bill give her hand a squeeze and instead of saying the first thought that had come into her mind, she took a deep breath and let out a sigh "I'm open to opportunities" Ally replied.

"What opportunities?" a voice asked behind her. Ally froze – she hoped Hugh hadn't heard that, "nothing Monkey." Sally gave Ally a puzzled look "if your mom would have another man" Sally said with Ally glaring at her. "Of course she will, dad's love has transformed, we are just waiting to meet him, but I don't think we will be waiting long" Hugh alleged. Ally's eyes shot across to where Hugh stood but before she could ask anything more Hugh and Aden had quickly picked up their ropes and run to the bale of hay.

"What is that Monkey dreaming up?" Ally wondered as she recalled that everything Hugh had asked for so far had come true. Ally downed the rest of her glass of wine, Helen leant across and poured her another glass. Sally wasn't letting this one go, she had got the bit between her teeth. "So what would your dream man be like" she asked. "Come on you, that's enough of your match making" John interrupted, seeing how uncomfortable Ally had become. Sally turned to John "I was only asking" she said innocently and then turned back to Ally, "so…"

Ally took another gulp of wine "I don't know to be honest…alive I guess", they chuckled at her remark. "You must have an idea" said Sally, clearly not satisfied with Ally's dismissive comment. Ally knew Sally wasn't going to let it drop until she felt she had got an answer. "What the hell" Ally said, putting her glass on the table and raising he hands to the sky, "tall, dark and handsome." Sally looked at her "this isn't a fairy tale…come on, just describe your dream man" Sally pleaded. Ally looked back up at the stars and let her mind begin to build a picture of her dream man "well, I guess he would be kind, caring, good at co-creating, I would get that funny feeling in my stomach, not nervous butterflies, but butterflies of happiness, he would be accomplished and know what he wanted to achieve in his life, and when we kissed it would be incredible and I'd get that feeling we're both one."

Ally looked back at everyone sitting around the table. Sally smiled proudly; everyone was captivated by the picture of the dream man she had described. "He has to get past me first", Bill said protectively as he had taken Ally and Hugh under his wing. Helen laughed "that won't be hard". Everyone began to laugh, and Bill sat back in his seat pretending to sulk. "He sounds incredible" Sally said as the laughter began to die off. "He will be – I won't settle for anything less, I'll know when I meet him." Ally sat back, satisfied that no one could fulfil her criteria.

As they were pouring the last of the wine, Hugh and Aden returned with their arms aching from roping. "None for me" Sally said, "we'd best be making tracks" as she looked across at John and Aden. "Yeah I think you're right" John replied. Everyone got up "thanks for coming" Ally said giving them both a hug. "Thanks for the ace stew" John said. "Come on you" John said, scooping Aden under his arm. "Night" Hugh called to Aden, "see you tomorrow" Aden replied before disappearing off into the darkness.

"Right, you, time for bed" Ally said looking at Hugh who was struggling to keep his eyes open. Hugh sluggishly got off his chair, got his pyjamas out of the truck and went to get changed. Ally waited until he reappeared from inside the motor home and then they made their way to the back of the pickup. Ally lowered the back and Hugh climbed into the den they had made with the blankets, cushions and sleeping bags. "Night Monkey" Ally said, "night mom." Hugh gave her a hug and a kiss and wrapped himself in the sleeping bag. "Sweet dreams little man" Ally said closing the back of the truck.

Ally went to the passenger side of the truck and took out her diary. Closing the door she made her way back to the table. Bill and Helen were inside washing up the last of the glasses. Ally opened her diary and began to write as she sat under the stars:

Dear Diary,

Well I survived the first day! We watched some team roping and I got Hugh a rope as he is now aspiring to be the world champion. Next he'll be wanting a horse!

When we were at the roping stall we met Sally, John and Aden, and they joined us for dinner with Bill and Helen. It's been a while since I have cooked for others but I think I pulled it off, there wasn't any left which I guess is a good sign.

I thought I was going to die when Sally started asking about my dream man, but, you know, they're kind of right. I can't go around avoiding love, or happiness, just because I feel guilty, feeling that I shouldn't be happy now Hugh's dad is gone. He would have been proud of his boy today and of us coming on this trip. They're the things I need to be focusing on, and who knows, if wishes come true my dream man may sweep me off my feet. I'm not holding my breath, he has got big shoes to fill, and I am not letting just anyone into our lives.

I still feel Hugh's dad around me especially when I look at the stars. He's acting as our Northern star, guiding us each day. Would he really want to guide me to another man? It's not something we ever talked about. I guess I thought we didn't have to, that we would be together until we were old.

Anyway the day was good. I enjoyed the dinner tonight – bringing new friendships to life and nourishing our existing friendship with Bill and Helen. Who knows what tomorrow will bring? But like Bill suggested, I'm going to start being open to receiving the new opportunities life provides. I think Hugh is definitely onto something with this magic of life, there have definitely been one too many coincidences happening lately to not think someone is watching over us.

Love always

Ally

Ally closed the diary and placed it on the table as the peaceful feeling began to flow up from her feet all the way to her head. She heard Helen and Bill start to set up their bed, she scooped up the diary and poked her head through their door, "night", they both turned round "night" Bill said, "we'll see you in the morning." Ally put her diary in the front of the truck, then made her way round to the back and slowly lowered it trying not to wake Hugh and climbed in, pulling it closed behind her.

Ally opened the back of the pickup after a restless night's sleep from having a very strange dream. As she climbed out of the back of the pickup she was greeted by the buzz of the fair. Ally glanced across to the arenas – they were already in full swing. Ally made her way round to the table outside the motor home; Helen was sitting with a paper doing a crossword. "Morning sleepy" she said "did you sleep alright?" Ally started to make her way to the motor home door "not really, I couldn't get settled, I just kept having a really weird dream." Helen's eyebrows lifted, and with that Ally went to make herself a cup of tea.

She returned with a fresh steaming cup of tea and sat down. "Where is everyone?" she asked. Helen put her paper down "they are at the arenas, I'm not sure what they are watching, Hugh seemed to have it all figured out. Sally, John and Aden are with them too, they came by the motor home earlier on. I'm sure Hugh will be keeping an eye on Bill making sure he doesn't cause too much trouble" Helen said shaking her head at the thought of what her man was up to. "They said they would come back around tea time" Helen finished.

"What have you got planned for the day?" Helen asked Ally. "Well, to be honest, not a lot. I think I am just going to relax here, maybe read a bit. I'm going to take full advantage of the free child care" Ally chuckled. "That sounds like a good plan to me" Helen said, picking up her coffee.

Hugh and Aden were up on top of the arena side to get the best view of the competitions, with Bill peering through the rails. Sally and John had gone for a wander around the shop stalls. "Did you see that?" Hugh said as a man jumped off his horse onto a cow. "Yeah we don't do it that way on the ranch" Aden replied. Hugh took out his timetable and looked at what was next. Aden peered across, "brilliant – team roping" Hugh said excitably. "Do you fancy heading up to the starting gates to get a better view?" Aden asked, "can we do that?" Hugh said, a little unsure. "Yeah course we can" Aden said climbing down. Aden turned to Bill, "we're going to head up to the starting stalls" he said, "good idea, I wonder if Steve is still working up there" Bill said, scanning the starting gate. "Who's Steve?" Hugh asked, "he's someone I knew way back when I was working at the ranches" Bill said as he started to walk towards the starting gate.

As they made their way through the crowd of people it quickly turned into a crowd of horses, with some cowboys sitting on the arena fence. Bill led the way.

As they reached the gate, Bill spotted Steve. They carried on going around to the other side of the arena, "Steve" Bill shouted to a man who was a similar age to Bill but slighter who lifted his head then smiled when he recognised who had called his name. They took each other's hands and shook them. "How are you doing mate" Steve said "not bad and yourself?" Bill asked "good, are they yours?" Steve said looking down at Hugh and Aden. "Oh no, just looking after them for the day" Bill said, ushering the boys closer. "Come here lads you can sneak through here and get a better view" Steve said pointing to a small gap in front of him that looked directly into the starting gate. The boys made their way over and got comfortable.

Bill and Steve were busy catching up with what they had been up to for the last few years. When the first riders took their position the commentator announced the cowboy's name followed by the horse's name, and then they were off as the first cow left the shoot. One after the other went through; the boys didn't say a word as they were mesmerized by it all. Then a horse and cowboy took the box closest to them. Hugh recognised the horse from the day before. It was the bay mare with the blonde streaks in her mane. The commentator introduced the pair as Ben and his horse Firefly. The guy nodded his head, with Tom on red rock, and then they were off. They were the quickest by far as Ben roped the head and Tom got the heels of the cow.

Bill and Steve had stopped talking to watch. Steve turned to Bill "that's Ben, he's a good hand, he has a ranch a few hours away, got some real nice cattle." Bill nodded in acknowledgement. As the next contestants entered, Ben and Tom made their way round to the back of the start gates to where Steve and Bill were standing. Steve turned to Ben "that's a damn good time, are you going for the championships?", "it's worth a try" Ben smiled.

Hugh had moved away from where he had been stood with Aden. He went over to Bill and Steve, he lifted his hand "hey Firefly" he said rubbing the horse's forehead. The mare lowered her head to Hugh's height, "she'll keep you there all day" Ben said reaching and rubbing the mare on the neck. "How old is she?" Hugh enquired, "just coming up six, she's doing well at the moment" Ben said. "Do you ride?" he said looking down at Hugh, "a little but not since my dad died as my mum stopped spending so much time with the horses and riding, she only went to feed and water them in the end" Hugh said stepping closer to Firefly's shoulder. He reached up and put his arms round her neck and took a deep breath in, he had missed the smell of the horses.

"Do you want a go?" Ben said, getting off Firefly, "she's a real gentle mare." Hugh looked at Bill to see if it was ok, Bill smiled "your mom doesn't need to know everything we get up to today, I won't tell her if you don't" he said with a twinkle in his eye. Hugh lifted his leg and his toe just reached the stirrup, Bill came behind and lifted him up. Hugh swung his leg over the other side. He shuffled in the western saddle and looked around him, his smile grew, Ben handed him the reins. "Left, right, stop and back" he said moving Hugh's hands in different directions.

"You ok?" Ben asked looking up at Hugh on Firefly. "Ok? This is awesome!" Hugh exclaimed. Everyone laughed as Hugh squeezed his legs together and Firefly began to walk forward. "Just walk around us in a big old circle" Ben began. Hugh sat back trying to imitate the other cowboys around him, "that's it, now try a stop" Ben instructed. Hugh lifted up the reins and moved them towards his belly button. Firefly slowed down and stopped her feet. Hugh burst into a laugh of pure ecstasy. "Do you know how to rope?" Ben asked "a little, we were practising last night" Hugh replied pointing at Bill and Aden. "Alright then" Ben said, lifting his rope up and passing it over to Hugh, "have your reins loose in your left hands with your coils, then spin your loop with your right hand, but be careful not to spank Firefly" Ben said taking a step back and grabbing a bin that was nearby. "Right, rope the bin" Ben suggested.

Hugh squeezed Firefly into walk and circled around so he was in front of the bin. He built his loop and swung it three times and let go. The rope landed on

Firefly's ears, she shook her head and the loop fell to the ground. Ben smiled and just as he was about to say something Hugh shouted "oh bugger, I didn't open my left hand!" He re-coiled the rope and Ben took a step back. Hugh walked Firefly on, and brought her to a stop. He built a loop, one, two, three swings and let the loop soar through the air. It landed just to the right of the bin.

"Now you're getting the hang of it" Ben said, sinking his hands into his pockets. Hugh set off again and this time the loop flew past the bin. "Right, this is going to be the one" Hugh said with determination. As Firefly was doing her circle Hugh began to build his loop and then brought her to a stop in front of the bin. He swung the rope and let go – the loop travelled through the air and landed around the bin. Hugh stood up in his stirrups "yahoo! I'm the world champion!" Everyone clapped and cheered.

Ben walked towards the bin and lifted off the rope. He walked towards Firefly and Hugh, "it looks like I've got stiff competition to win the championships this year" Ben said handing over the rope. "Don't worry, I'll let you have this championships" Hugh said cheekily, then laughed. "Right, I had better go and put Firefly away in her stall – she's worked hard today" Ben said. Hugh leant forward and gave Firefly a big hug "thanks Firefly" he whispered then slid off the saddle and came round to Firefly's nose to give her a kiss.

Hugh turned round to Ben and gave him a hug. "Thanks Ben, that was out of this world", "anytime" Ben said reaching down and hugging him back. Ben put his foot in the stirrup and swung back up into the saddle. He steered Firefly to the left and Tom motioned for his horse to follow. Hugh went over to where Bill was standing. Beaming from ear to ear, he didn't know what to say to explain the bucket loads of happiness he was feeling right now.

Bill smiled back, knowing what Hugh was trying to say. "Mom, Dad" Aden called as he saw his parents walk past them. Sally and John spun round to see, Hugh, Bill, Aden and Steve standing together. "Hey guys, how was your afternoon?" Sally asked. They looked at each other, Hugh spoke up first "it was amazing, I got to rope and ride one of the horses." His hands flung to his mouth. "But you can't tell mom" he said sheepishly, "don't worry we won't" John said with a wink.

"Come on Hugh we're missing the action" Aden said, making his way back to the arena. Bill said goodbye to Steve and then followed Sally, John, Hugh and Aden to the arena side where they spent the rest of the afternoon.

Bill, Helen, Ally and Hugh sat around the table having dinner. Hugh was just finishing his last mouthful, "mom do you want to go to the stage tonight and listen to the live bands?" Ally leant back in her chair, "yeah that'll be good, do you know who's playing", "no, but they can't be that bad if they are playing here" Hugh said. Ally smiled "I guess not, let me just have a shower and we'll head over, are you guys coming?" looking at Bill and Helen. "No I think we're going to hit the bar tonight" Bill said looking for Helen's approval, she nodded in agreement.

"I'll use the shower first" Hugh said picking up his plate and heading into the motor home. Ally sat back in her chair. She had had such a chilled out day doing nothing and it felt great, a 'sharpening the saw' day she thought. I'm sure Hugh has got the rest of the days jam-packed with stuff to do. Then Hugh reappeared dressed and showered ready to head off to the stage, "that was quick" Ally remarked, Hugh smiled, "the shower's free mom." Ally got the hint, Hugh wanted to head off.

Ally grabbed some clean clothes and her wash bag and headed into the bathroom. Bill and Helen collected the rest of the dirty pots and went inside to wash up. Hugh got his travel bag out of the car and took out his diary:

Dear Dan the Diary,

I've got to tell you about the most incredible thing I did today. I have been wanting to tell someone all day but I can't tell mom because she would go mad. We were watching the team roping and Bill knew a guy called Steve near the starting gates, and we went to see him and get a closer look at the roping. While we were there we met Ben and Tom, and Ben let me ride his horse called Firefly and I roped a bin. I was rubbish to start with but I roped it after a few attempts. I love Firefly so much that I think she should be my horse; I miss riding and the horses. Ben is really nice – I think mom and him would get on really well. All the things I am asking for are coming true. I circle a place on the map that I want to go to and then add notes about my dreams coming true, then I meet the people who help it to come true, this trip is amazing! I think mom is starting to remember the magic of life too. I have circled Ben's ranch on the map which is the next place we are going to go to. I wish that me and mom could spend some time on Ben's ranch. I would like to ride with him and rope cattle, and I wish I was a team roping champion too. Anyway, mom's ready now. We're going to listen to the bands playing on the stage.

Hugh

Hugh put his diary back in his travel bag and placed it on the back seat of the car. As he shut the door he saw his mom standing there wearing her cowgirl boots, jeans, a sparkly top and a demon jacket. "You look great mom!" Hugh said. Ally looked down at the outfit she had decided to wear "you know what, Monkey, I feel great too."

"Don't worry mom I'll fight off the cowboys" Hugh joked. Bill stuck his head out of the motor home door and wolf whistled. Helen joined him "on the pull are we?" she joked. Ally smiled – nothing anyone said tonight would bring her out of this good feeling. "Come on Hugh, let's find this music" Ally said taking hold of Hugh's hand.

They made their way through the cars, past the arenas and then they heard the band in the distance. Hugh moved closer so as not to lose his mom. Ally weaved through the crowd towards a small clearing where they stood to take in the surroundings. They stared up at the stage; the music was blasting out of the speakers. Hugh looked around the crowd for anyone he knew but didn't spot anyone. He looked up at Ally, watching her sway to the beat of the music; she had always loved to dance. He smiled and wrapped his arms around her waist – it was great to see her so happy again he thought. Ally reached down and put her arm around Hugh's shoulder. The next song came on and as the catchy beat grew louder Ally looked at Hugh "may I have this dance?" she said in an old English accent. "Of course you may" Hugh replied, bending forward in a swaggering bow. They began to dance, twirling round, twisting, side stepping and pulling funny faces.

They laughed at each other, but it felt so good. They continued through the next two songs and then Ally made a time out sign with her hands, as she was trying to catch her breath. Ally sat down on the grass. Hugh had another look around the crowd and his gaze stopped at three men standing a little way back behind them. He squinted through the darkness and then recognised Ben's face. "Mom I'm just going to say hi to some friends I met today", "ok I'll wait here" Ally replied as she sat swaying to the music.

Hugh ran over to where Ben and Tom were stood. "Hi Ben" he said as ran up to them, out of breath. "Hey champion, how you doing?" Ben asked "I'm good, who's this" pointing at a man stood next to Tom. "That's Chad" Ben said taking a sip of his beer. Hugh walked over to where Chad was standing. "Hi I'm Hugh" he said, holding out his hand. Chad reached and shook it "I'm Chad nice to meet ya." Hugh walked back to Ben and stood in front of him. Ben took his eyes off the stage and looked at Hugh "how is Firefly?" Hugh asked, concerned. "She's fine, happy eating her hay, she has got a big day tomorrow" Ben replied, and looked at Tom, and then back at the stage. "Are you going to win the championship tomorrow?" Hugh asked. Tom stepped in "he has won it for the past two years, another year wouldn't hurt." Ben just smiled at him in response to his comment.

"How many horses do you have?" Hugh asked "Steve told me you had a ranch a few hours away and that you have really nice cattle there." Ben knelt down, giving Hugh his full attention "we've got about 60 horses and 1500 cattle at the ranch" Ben replied. "Is Firefly your favourite horse?" asked Hugh "she is definitely mine and I know she is going to win the championships tomorrow" Hugh concluded. "She's one of my favourites too, and thanks for the heads up, I think she'll do great tomorrow too" Ben said, standing back up.

Ben looked at Hugh – it was his turn to ask the questions. "Who was that you were dancing with?" as he looked across at the woman who had caught his eye and stirred his heart. "Oh that's my mom, we are on an adventure." Hugh began to tell Ben about his vision wall, coming on this trip, meeting Janet, Bill and Helen and then meeting Aden, Sally and John. Hugh pulled out his map "see, here are the places we have been and people we have met, and here are the dreams that have come true" he said pointing to a circle with writing in it on the corner of the map.

Ben studied the map. "Why have you circled the town where my ranch is?" Ben enquired. "Because that's where we are heading after the fair" Hugh said casually. "Does your mom know that?" Ben asked. "Not yet but I'll tell her before we set off. She is just remembering how magical life is and she is starting to be happy again like she used to be so I don't want to scare her with all my plans. I'll let her know nearer the time, anyway, she said she wanted to take it one day at a time. Maybe we could visit you and Firefly?" Hugh said looking hopefully up at Ben. "Well you're both more than welcome. I have a BBQ back at the ranch every year after the fair – you and your mom are welcome to come." "We'll be there" Hugh said, jumping on the spot, "anyway I had better get back to mom."

Hugh put the map away in his pocket and said goodbye to Tom, Chad and Ben and walked across to where Ally was sitting. He sat down beside her. "Are you alright Monkey?" Ally asked, "great mom! This is the best trip ever" Hugh said leaning against her. "I second that" Ally said, wrapping her arms around Hugh.

6 THE BAR

The next two days went by very fast as Hugh darted from arena to arena, not wanting to miss a minute of everything that was happening. As the last day of the fair arrived Hugh was up early and woke Ally up too. "Come on mom, it's the finals." They got dressed and headed over to the arena where they spent the day watching the competitions and some of the prize-giving ceremonies.

As the evening neared Ally took Hugh's hand as they walked up the steps into the bar. Hugh's attention was still on the arena, watching the rodeo riders. "Excuse me" Ally said as they slid through a group of people standing around the entrance to the bar. Ally's stomach did a big rumble in protest at not having any food all day. "Come on, Monkey, it's time for some food." There was no response as Hugh was trying to keep the arena in view as the door began to close and it gradually disappeared.

Ally looked at the barman "do you do food?" He nodded towards the menus stood up on the table, "oh great, thanks" Ally responded. "Ok, Monkey, what do you want? I think I'm going to have a steak, I can't fit another burrito in my stomach" Ally said whilst scanning the menu. Hugh had a quick glance "can I have chips and pie mom", "what's the magic word?" Ally teased, "pleeeease!!!!" Hugh said cheekily. "What drink would you like with that?" Ally asked, getting up from the table. "Orange please" Hugh said whilst trying to peer out of the window to catch a glimpse of what was happening in the arena.

Ally walked up to the bar, placed the order and brought the drinks back to the table. "So, Hugh, what has been your favourite bit so far?" Hugh shuffled in his seat to get comfy ready to tell his story. Ally placed her elbows on the table and cupped her head with her hands ready in anticipation.

As Hugh was in full swing telling his story about the adventures that day the food arrived but that didn't disrupt his flow, he carried on between chews. When he finished his meal, he wrapped up his story. "Mom isn't it great how the timing of life is just perfect? The lessons don't arrive too fast so you don't become overwhelmed but fast enough to keep things interesting. And just look at how much fun you can fit into a day!" Ally smiled "I guess so." Hugh then turned to survey the room, looking at the pictures hanging on the wall and the people sitting at the tables. Ally began to collect the dishes and take them to the bar as she saw Hugh climb down off his stool and wander over to the other side of the room.

As Ally was walking over to the bar she heard a familiar tune start to play, then a familiar voice, "mom, mom, mom!" Hugh's shouting was getting progressively louder. "It's our song! Come on, quick!" Hugh was standing in the middle of the empty dance floor, arms poised and feet ready for dancing.

Ally placed the plates on the bar and looked at the barman. He nodded in acknowledgement and Ally started to make her way to the dance floor. Ally smiled to herself at Hugh's bursting confidence in doing whatever made him feel happy even if it was sometimes a little unconventional. Ally scooped Hugh up in her arms and let the music take them both on a journey of happiness as they spun around the dance floor. "Where the brave are free and lovers soar…life is a highway, I wanna drive it all night long" Hugh began singing at the top of his voice. Ally couldn't stop laughing at how happy and free she felt. Free from fear, free from worry and, most of all, free to feel unconditional love. No sooner had the song begun it came to an end.

Ally put Hugh back on the ground and watched him walk off. Whilst dancing, Hugh had spotted Ben, Tom and Chad sitting on the other side of the dance floor and he made his way over to them. "Hi guys" he said as he reached the table. "What a coincidence seeing you here" Tom said. Hugh smiled "no such thing, just perfect timing." Ally headed back to their table and pulled out her tablet. She couldn't avoid checking her emails and checking in on reality any longer, the never-ending job list she mumbled to herself.

As her emails were downloading Ally glanced up to see where Hugh was. She looked across the dance floor and spotted Hugh at a table were three men were sitting. Hugh was holding one of their ropes and swinging it around; she overheard one of the men saying "and here we have the champion roper." As Hugh let go of the loop and watched it gently land over the stool he said "my mom always watches the roping at home, she thinks I don't notice, but she gets really excited as they rope the cows, maybe one day she will pick up a rope again and have a go on horseback like I did with Firefly." Ben looked at Hugh "maybe she should put it in her dream circle on her map." Hugh laughed "my mom used to believe in all that stuff and was lots of fun, talking about dreams which always seemed to come true, creating and having happiness as her default setting, but when dad died she forgot, but I'm helping her to remember.

Like the other night she described her dream man, and I know she'll meet him one day." Ben sat back in his seat and looked up to where Ally was sitting "maybe she will" he whispered.

Ally looked at her tablet: 205 emails, seriously! "Well that serves me right for not checking them for over a week" Ally rubbed her face "the world's spinning so fast nowadays that there's no time to enjoy the moment! Well, I had better make a start on them" Ally said to herself.

Ally was just starting to work through the emails when she heard a bang. Her head shot up – "Hugh?!" Hugh was looking straight at Ally, "busted" he thought. The rope was wrapped around the table, which was now laying on its side with its contents sprawled on the floor. Ally sighed as she slid her bar stool back and made her way over to where Hugh was standing. She felt the barman's eyes burn into her back with disapproval as she walked over to Hugh. One of the men had already got up and was standing the table back up. "I'm really sorry mom I was just practising, I didn't mean for it to fall over" Hugh said apologetically. "Don't worry son just pick up the salt and pepper for me", Ally said whilst she bent down and began to unravel the rope from the table legs. She coiled the rope back up and handed it back to the man who stood next to the table. Ally looked back over her shoulder at Hugh "come on, Monkey, time

to sit down for a bit and leave these men in peace",
"oh don't worry mam, he's no trouble and this was
my fault, I suggested roping the table" Ben said.

Ally looked back at the man standing in front of her.
He was taller than she had expected and she thought
he must be a ranch worker with his checked shirt and
cowboy hat. Her eyes carried on wandering down.
Hmm wranglers too with a large belt buckle showing
a man roping. She carried on down to his cowboy
boots, scuffed and dirty. They looked like they had
been worn for many hours, she noticed the leather
was creased and well broken in. The man's voice
broke her vetting of him "hi, my name is Ben", and
put his hand out. Ally realised she had been checking
him over a moment too long. "Hi I'm Ally" as she
took hold of his hand and they shook. She looked up
and made eye contact with Ben "wow, what beautiful
eyes" she thought.

The other two men who were sitting around the table
stood up and held out their hands "hi I'm Tom" "and
I'm Chad." Ally turned and took their hand one at a
time "hi, I'm Ally, nice to meet you." Then silence fell
like a damp mist over a valley. Ally shuffled from side
to side "well um, Hugh, let's head back to the table."
Ben hadn't taken his eyes off Ally "you're more than
welcome to join us" Ben spoke up, his voice warm
and kind. Ally froze as a thousand thoughts started
racing through her head as she stared at Ben. Hugh

stepped in "ok, I'll just get our stuff." As Hugh made his way across the dance floor Ally's daze broke, she had one last check over Ben and the guys, quietly deliberating whether she could trust them, and then went to collect her belongings.

As she was packing her tablet into her bag she whispered to Hugh "if at any point you start to feel unsafe around these guys just let me know and we'll leave straight away", "don't worry mom I know these guys, I met them a few days ago with Bill, John, Sally and Aden. Anyway, my gut feeling is that we were meant to meet them, they're part of our journey." Hugh was trying not to spill the beans about riding and roping with Firefly. Ally paused and then she shook her head. Why did she still get surprised by these moments? Of course Hugh knew them, and of course they were part of the journey. Why else would Hugh be speaking to them? She put her tablet back into her bag, "where does he get his wisdom from?" she asked herself. Ally picked up her drink and followed Hugh's footprints across the dance floor to the other side of the room to where Ben, Tom and Chad were sitting and Hugh was pulling up a chair.

Ally pulled a chair up next to Hugh and Chad, opposite Ben and Tom. Hugh had already picked up the rope and was inspecting the honda. The bar had started to fill up with people and a buzz began to float around the room. Ally glanced across to a small stage where she could hear a band setting up, moving speakers and laying out cable.

Ally turned to Chad "do you know who's playing tonight?", "no afraid not, they were playing last night and from what the lads were saying" he nodded across to where Ben and Tom were sitting "they said they were pretty good." Ally nodded in acknowledgement as she turned her head back to the band and Chad started talking to Tom. Ally could hear Hugh asking Ben question after question about roping and Ben just kept answering them with no sign of frustration. "Hugh must have asked at least thirty questions by now; I wonder how long Ben will last the interrogation?" Ally chuckled to herself. "What's funny mom?" Hugh asked mid-question. Ally glanced down at her most precious gift "nothing Monkey", "hey mom, did you know Ben's a team roper?", "no I didn't, any good?" Ally said in jest. "He's only won the championships for the past two years, and he won it again today for the third time on his horse called Firefly. She's called that because of the blonde through her mane and tail" Hugh replied. Ally looked at Ben – she remembered seeing that horse on the first day. Her eyes drifted to a couple sitting on the other side of the dance floor. "He must be alright then" Ally mumbled before becoming lost in her thoughts, thinking about the first night at the fair and describing her dream man. She smiled to herself "not a chance, those things just don't happen."

Ben turned to Tom "well I think it's your turn to buy the round." Tom grumbled "it's always my turn." Ben and Chad laughed "tight as a duck's arse" they said in unison. "Same again?" Tom asked, pointing towards the bottles of beers on the table. "And an orange juice for me" Hugh piped up. Tom turned to Ally "what would you like?" Ally thought to herself "I wonder if they do any decent whiskys?" Hugh gave her a big cheesy grin "me and Aden are going to sleep in the back of the pickup tonight mom, with it being the last night." Ally's eyebrows raised "that's news to me!"

Ally looked at Tom "in that case a whisky straight." Tom looked a bit bemused "straight with ice and water?" Ally looked at him sternly "no just a glass with whisky in it, do you think you'll remember that or shall I write it in big letters for you?" Ally said sarcastically. Chad and Ben sniggered which quickly turned into belly roaring laughs. Tom smiled and made his way to the bar. Ally looked at the others – they tried to hide their laughter but it was no good. Chad was trying to say something but he couldn't form a sentence without laughing after the first word. Hugh looked at Ally "what's so funny about straight whisky?" Ally smiled "I don't think they were expecting it."

As Ben and Chad began to regain composure, Tom returned with the drinks and slid Ally's whisky across the table with a sceptical look. He placed Hugh's orange juice in front of him and made his way back to the bar to collect the bottles of beer. As Tom returned Ally lifted the glass to her lips and let the sweet nectar soothe her body as it glided down her throat. Ben, Chad and Tom were all watching, surprised at Ally's expression of pure bliss. "Cheers!" Hugh called, everyone lifted their glass and clinked "cheers!"

There was a strum on the guitar as the band started their sound check. Ally saw a little boy whizz across the dance floor skidding to a halt using Hugh as a crash mat. "Aden!" Hugh exclaimed, Ally turned in her seat and saw Sally and John making their way over. Ally stood up and gave them both a big hug "hi, how are you doing? How was your day?" she asked. Ally's attention was suddenly diverted over to where Hugh was building a loop "hey Hugh no roping indoors, there are too many people in here now", "ok mom we're going outside then." Hugh and Aden turned to start making their way across the dance floor. "Hang on a minute, don't you need to ask someone if it's ok if you can take the rope outside?" Hugh paused and looked at Ben, Ben leaned back in his seat and smiled. In that second the boys were off chatting away to each other while they ran. "What are we going to rope?" Ally heard Aden call, "everything!" Hugh replied.

Ally turned back to Sally who had now occupied Hugh's seat and John was just grabbing a chair from the next table to put next to Ben. Ally introduced everyone "this is Ben, Tom and Chad, and this is Sally and John", "hi, good to see you again" as they all shook hands. Sally looked at John, John sat still for a moment trying to de-code what that look meant. "Oh right" and stood up, "anyone want a drink?" Tom and Chad lifted up their bottles and tapped the air, not wanting to disrupt the flow of their conversation. Ben nodded too. John turned to Ally "straight whisky?" Ally smiled "why not" she replied. "Malibu and coke for you" looking towards Sally. Ben stood up "I'll give you a hand." Ally and Sally watched them as they walked towards the bar. "He's a hotty" Sally said smiling, Ally gave her a nudge with her shoulder and they chuckled. Their gaze drifted to the stage as the band started to sing their first song.

John and Ben returned with the drinks. Sally and Ally were swaying to the music. As John and Ben sat down they continued their conversation about the cattle and Sally joined in. Whilst everyone was deep in conversation Ally took the opportunity to slip away for a dance, she scanned the room for any eligible bachelors and her eyes met a cowboy leaning against a table watching people on the dance floor. Ally looked over at him and nodded towards the dance floor and he nodded back in agreement at Ally as she stood up and walked onto the dance floor. Ben's eyes diverted from the conversation as he watched Ally get up and move to the dance floor where a man was waiting. He returned back to the conversation with Sally and John but kept glancing at Ally as she moved around the floor.

Ally met the man on the dance floor and took hold of his hands, as they began to drift around the floor. She looked up with a nervous smile as she stood on his toe for the second time "sorry I'm a bit rusty" Ally said. He looked away trying to hide the throbbing pain in his toe. Just as Ally started to get into the swing of things the boys came hurtling across the dance floor with wide grins and bright eyes. "What have you guys been up to?" Sally asked whilst looking at their rosy red cheeks. "Roping" Aden said breathlessly. "Where's mom?" Hugh asked. "She's just dancing" Sally responded. Hugh scanned the dance floor for his mom and came across her looking uncomfortable shuffling around the dance floor.

"Mom!" he shouted. Ally looked across and saw Hugh. She excused herself and made her way over to where the group were sitting. Sally looked at her with one eyebrow raised. Ally shook her head "brutal, that's all I can say", "that's because it wasn't me" Hugh said, hugging his mom. Ben stood up "I'll get the next round in" and made his way to the bar as the boys climbed into his seat.

Ben returned to the group as Ally was talking with Sally about the next step of the adventure. Ben pulled up a chair behind the two of them. The smell of his aftershave surrounded Ally and smelt sweet. Ally took a deep breath in, letting the smell fill her body as she got goose bumps. "You're not heading off yet are you?" Ben enquired. Ally looked at him "no we're going to head to Yellowstone Park after the fair has gone." She became lost in his stunning eyes as their gaze held hers. "Oh right" Ben smiled to himself as he recalled the circle around his town on Hugh's map.

"Come on, mom, let's show them how it's supposed to be done!" Hugh said, grabbing Ally's hand, at the same time breaking her and Ben's gaze. Ben watched as Ally and Hugh walked onto the dance floor and began to swirl around the floor, laughing and singing. He smiled to himself "she sure is an incredible mom" he thought.

As the next song began Ally felt a hand on her shoulder. "Do you mind if I steal your mom for a dance?" Ben said, taking hold of Ally's hand. "No" and Hugh was off back to Aden as they started to plan the next objects they could rope. Ben brought Ally in closer to him, Ally looked up and then broke eye contact immediately. She felt like a little school girl dancing with her crush. As soon as that thought crossed her mind "crush!" she thought, "what crush?! Hang on a moment." She was just about to give herself a talking to when Ben spun her around and Ally began to laugh and relax into his arms. "Just for this moment I'm free to live my dream" she thought.

The song came to an end and Ally got ready to move back to the table but Ben stood there holding her hand waiting for the next song to begin. They danced and laughed as the band kept playing. All Ally's barriers melted away in that moment. She laid her head on his chest as a slow song came on, allowing her dream to become reality. Ally glanced across and caught sight of the group sitting watching them. As the song was coming to an end Ally was just about to make a time out sign with her hands when the band announced they were going to have a short break. Ben placed his hand on her lower back, guiding her back to everyone. As they walked they chuckled about each other's dancing.

Ally asked "where are the boys?" "Outside – they are making roping videos" Sally said, smirking at what she had just witnessed between Ally and Ben. Ally nodded in response, trying to avoid the inevitable conversation of Sally saying "I told you so". Ben found an empty seat and Ally moved to a seat opposite him. Everyone was deep in conversation. Ally checked her phone for any missed calls from Hugh and glanced up. She made eye contact with Ben and then looked away quickly as she could not stop herself from smiling every time she saw him. Ally looked back at her phone, no missed calls, "I had better go and check on them" she thought.

"Who wants another drink?" Ally asked and everyone nodded in agreement. Ally looked at Sally "I'll just check on the boys too." Sally nodded "yeah they've been out there for a while, they have probably tied themselves up in knots," they both chuckled.

Ally made her way to the bar entrance, stuck her head out of the door and spotted the boys standing on barrels trying to rope each other. "Hugh! Aden! Do you want a drink?" Ally shouted. The boys looked up, jumped off the barrels and came running over "yes please" Aden replied, "oh yes please mom" Hugh said. The three of them made their way over to the bar. Between them they scooped up the drinks and took them across to the table. As Ally placed Chad's and Tom's bottles down she looked for an empty seat. Aden and Hugh were already showing Sally and John the films they had just made. Ben caught Ally's attention and motioned to a free space next to him. Ally slid down and let out a sigh of relief. She felt all the past year's stress and tension leave her body. Ben looked at her and smiled.

Sally broke the silence as she watched the boy's films. "Oh, hey, who's that pretty little thing in the dress?" Aden blushed and Hugh grinned. "Oh that's Jenny – she's our special friend." Everyone looked at each other and smiled – the joy of naivety. Hugh turned to

Ally with a serious look. Ally knew where this was going. As Hugh prepared one of his questions about life, Ally sat up in preparation and had another sip of her drink.

"Mom what does it feel like to kiss someone?" Hugh asked then looked at Sally with a mischievous smile. Ally's face reddened. She glanced down at the table trying to compose herself, then she started to recall the moment of her first kiss with Hugh's dad. Her mind began to settle as she played back the memory. Would she every get to experience that again? she thought. "Mom!" Hugh urged a reply. Ally came back to reality. Everyone had stopped their conversations and were looking at Ally waiting intently for her response. "Well, Hugh, the best way I can describe it is when your lips meet, the touch of the skin sends bubbles of happiness dancing in your belly, then your blood turns into liquid joy that flows around your whole body and then if it's really special you reach a moment when your bodies become one, and there is no separation between you and then all there is is love."

Everyone was silent. Hugh looked at his mom satisfied with her answer "it sounds incredible mom." Hugh looked at Sally and winked "mom does Ben kiss like that?" he asked. Ally was distant as she was still reliving the moment with Hugh's dad in her mind. "I don't know about that" Ally said, purposely avoiding eye contact with Ben. She sat up straight, determined not to let her fears take hold, "he may be a roping champion, but I don't think he is capable of a proper ten out of ten kiss" Ally said jokily. However, there was part of her which was curious but she dismissed the feeling. "So you don't think Ben would get ten out of ten mom?" Hugh was eager not to let the moment of opportunity pass but Ally ignored him. Ben put his beer down and stepped in "well, hang on a moment Hugh and I'll let you know the verdict." At that moment Ben reached round, gently placed his hand on the back of Ally's head and moved in for a kiss. It wasn't until Ben's lips were in full embrace that Ally realised what was happening. Before she could even move away the bubbles of happiness began, oh how she missed this! Then before she knew it the joy began to flow around her body, and her body began to tingle as every cell danced with love. Very suddenly Ben moved away.

Ally's face was a perfect picture of shock and disbelief as she felt something she didn't think she was ever going to feel again. Ben's eyes watched as he saw Ally trying to figure out her feelings, he watched as he realised something, the same realisation he had had when he had first seen her dancing with Hugh. Everyone was looking at Ally awaiting the verdict. Ally suddenly shuffled uncomfortably in her seat. "Well, nothing special" she lied, knowing full well that what just happened was something incredible. "I'd say a 7.5" she said, still flustered. The bubbles began to melt away and the joy left her blood as confusion and conflict wrapped around her chest like a corset one size too small.

Ben's eyes shone with satisfaction. "7.5 you say, that kiss was only 7.5, hmmm, where did the 2.5 go?" Ally looked at him and she couldn't stop the words stampeding out of her mouth. "It wasn't long enough, oh, what I mean is it had many flaws. That's just one. As I said, it was nothing special." Everyone burst into laughter at Ally as she tried to hide the amazing feeling it had given her, as they had witnessed the moment of love being shared. "Time for whisky" Ally scooted out of her seat and headed to the bar. Ben smiled as he knew the moment that he had just shared with Ally was a moment that he would never forget as he felt true love for the first time.

There was a ring of the bell as the barman shouted last orders. Ally was watching Aden and Hugh dancing around the floor. She enjoyed watching the young people with their bundles of energy, care free and no worries to weigh down their young shoulders. As the ring of the barman's bell ran through her body she sat up in her seat trying to bring her body back to the living and began to gather her things. Tom and Chad had already moved onto another bar looking for some 'fine fillies' as they put it.

Ben was still sitting next to Ally making sure he didn't lose his prize position all night. He had his arm draped casually on the back of Ally's seat while he was talking with Sally and John about his ranch only a few hours' drive away. Ally called across to Hugh "come on little man, it's time to call it a night", "oh mom, come on, it's too early" he pleaded. "Too early!" Ally responded sarcastically, "it's way past your bed time, and you're on breakfast duties in the morning." Hugh started to make his way across the dance floor to the table with Aden following behind him. "Can me and Aden sleep in the back of the truck tonight?" Ally stood up and then sat back down again quickly as her legs hadn't woken up yet. She looked up at Sally and John for their ok. Sally turned to Aden "as long as you go straight to sleep as soon as you get to the truck, and don't go wandering around the fair or roping."

The boys leapt into action collecting their things and made their way to the door. Ally stood back up as her legs began to function again and got ready to follow the two boys. As she moved away from the table and began to walk across the dance floor, she felt an arm wrap around her lower back. She looked to her right and there was Ben still talking to Sally and John like this was the most ordinary thing in the world.

Ally sighed – part of her was impressed with his sly moves and confidence but another part of her was doing somersaults of worry thinking about all the 'what ifs'. She sighed again, "I'm too tired to have this kind of debate with myself" she thought. She carried on to the door, they stepped outside and the cool night air sent a shiver down her body as she wrapped her arms around herself. Ben pulled her in closer.

As they reached the truck Hugh and Aden were putting out the sleeping bags and pillows, making a den in the back of the truck. "Night mom" Aden said, giving his mom a hug and kiss, and then moved onto his dad "night dad", "night son" John replied in a warm embrace. "Night mom" Hugh said "night superstar" Ally replied kissing him on the forehead. Hugh then moved onto Ben. "Night Ben" wrapping his arms around his waist, "night Hugh" Ben responding wrapping his arms around the little boy. Then the two boys disappeared into the back of the truck. The click of the back closing sent the boys into hushed whispers.

Ally hugged Sally "goodnight, see you for breakfast", "you bet ya" Sally added squeezing Ally tight and giving her a wink of approval of the night's events. Ally then moved onto John, "night John" John gave her a big bear hug and a squeeze "night Ally." Then the two of them walked off into the darkness back to their tent. Ally looked at Ben "well I guess good night then." Ben smiled "I'm not letting you off that easily, I still haven't got full marks for my kisses." Ally chuckled and looked up to the stars "he sure is persistent" she thought. And then her heart took over and she wrapped her arms around his neck and felt Ben's arms wrap around her waist. He pulled Ally in close. As their lips met it sent butterflies fluttering around her heart, and before she knew it their bodies merged into one and the love flowed. Ally didn't know how long the kiss lasted, all she knew was that it was perfect, he was perfect. Then out of nowhere Ben picked her up and spun her around in circles, Ally laughed in ecstasy.

Ben begrudgingly put Ally back down and gave her one more kiss before saying goodnight. He walked away "night Ben" Ally replied softly, and walked to the passenger side of the car. She put the seat back flat and grabbed a sleeping bag, wrapping it around her and slid into the chair. Maybe there is something to this dreaming she thought as she pulled out her diary.

Dear Diary,

What an incredible night! Me and Hugh went to the bar for some food, and Hugh introduced me to some friends he had made: Ben, Chad and Tom. Well as I later found out, Ben had let Hugh ride his horse and do some roping. He's really nice and, of course, Hugh had it all planned and was helping to create an opportunity for us to get together.

When we kissed it was incredible, he was perfect, and the more I find out about him the more things I like about him. But my head is screaming 'Stop! You'll just get hurt again, and go back to the way you felt before you left', but my heart is saying 'just allow the opportunity for love to transform.' I'm so confused about what to do. Oh well, I probably won't see him again anyway. But when he takes me in his arms I feel the way I felt when Hugh's dad was alive – that anything is possible, that life is just a series of joyful moments and adventures.

I guess tomorrow we'll go our separate ways as he heads off back to his ranch and we head to Yellowstone, but I can't help wonder 'what if?' Hugh keeps saying ask and it is given, so here goes.

I ask to not lose that feeling of love that returned tonight and give me the courage to listen to the whispers of my heart and follow my gut feelings, to allow the opportunities for my dreams to come true.

Love always

Ally

Ally closed her diary and put it on the back seat; she wrapped the sleeping bag tighter around her body and closed her eyes, replaying the night's events as she drifted off into the land of dreams. As Ben walked back to his truck he sunk his hands deep into his pockets, as he smiled to himself, he truly felt like a champion, winning the best prize in the world.

7 ARRIVING AT THE BBQ

As they were driving along the highway Ally looked to her right at Hugh who was busy watching his roping films that he had made with Aden. Ally could hear them on the film shouting instructions to each other and screams of joy when they roped whatever object they were aiming for. Ally looked back at the road in disbelief – she couldn't believe that they had talked her into doing this but part of her was excited to spend some time with Ben, not that she would admit that to herself.

That morning when she awoke, the boys where already up making breakfast with Sally and John whilst Bill and Helen were beginning to pack up. Ally rolled back over in the car seat, pulling up the sleeping bag and trying to disguise the fact that it was daylight. She was trying not to wake from the most incredible dream but before she had time to drift back to sleep the car door opened letting in a gust of cold air. Ally pulled the sleeping bag around her tighter "here you go mom" Hugh said, thrusting a glass of orange juice at her. Ally peeled back the sleeping bag and took the glass "thank you Hugh."

Hugh went back to the cooking stove; Aden was laying the table. Ally looked across at everyone. There was just Sally, John, Bill and Helen. Part of her was relieved but she couldn't help feeling a bit disappointed that Ben wasn't there. As she swung her legs out of the door, Tom and Chad came round from the back of the truck. "Morning" they said tipping their hats to Ally, "morning" Ally responded groggily.

Ally managed to slide from the car seat across to a camping chair where she flopped. "Way too much effort" she said to herself. Sally piped up "good morning, sunshine, it's a beautiful day, the sun is shining" in a loud chirpy voice. Ally rubbed her face with her hands "it's too early for that." Bill laughed as he looked at Ally. "I'll make you a cup of tea mom, that always makes you feel better" Ally gave Hugh a weary smile "thanks Hugh, I'd appreciate that."

Ally closed her eyes again as the sun was too bright and let her head rest on the back of the chair. Then she felt a kiss on her cheek, her eyes shot open, it was Ben. "Morning Miss Ally" he smiled with bright eyes.

Ally couldn't get any words to leave her mouth – she looked across to where Bill and Helen were sitting. "Don't worry, we have been filled in on last night's antics" Bill said chuckling. "Something smells good boys" Ben moved across to where the boys where serving up breakfast. Not only did the shock of the kiss bother Ally but her next thought filled her with fear, "what the hell do I look like?" She shuffled back in the seat to try to look at the reflection in the truck. Her eyes scanned her reflection but then her belly rumbled and she slid back down in her seat "I'm too tired to be bothered about that right now."

She felt a warm plate on her lap along with the smell of bacon. Her son was most definitely a legend, "there you go mom" Hugh also handed her a cup of tea, "you'll feel better after that" he smiled. Ally looked at the plate, the bacon sandwich looked perfect, as she took her first bite. Ally looked around – everyone was packing up and leaving as the fair had come to an end. Sally and John were looking at the map. Tom was talking with Chad about dropping a few horses off at his ranch and Ben was inviting them to the end of fair BBQ at his ranch. "Thanks mate but we're going to have to give it a miss this year, I need to get back" Tom said.

Ally's bacon sandwich didn't last long. As she supped her tea she began to feel human again. After listening to everyone talking about their plans she thought they had better start making theirs. "So, Hugh" Ally said placing her plate on the pile of dirty pots and heading to the back of the truck to fish out the map "where to next? Yellowstone?" Ally said turning back to the group. Sally avoided eye contact with Ally trying to hide her smirk. Tom and Chad took another bite out of their bacon sandwiches. "What did I miss?" Ally asked looking confused.

"Mom I have a plan" Hugh said, taking her hand and guiding her back to the empty chair. Ben put his plate down and dusted the crumbs off his jeans. "Well mom, you see, we've been talking" Hugh began. "Who's we?" Ally asked with eyebrows raised. "Me, Ben, Sally, John, Aden, Bill and Helen", "oh right, do I get to be part of this plan?" Ally asked inquisitively.

"Yes mom if you'd just let me finish" Ally raised her hands "sorry boss." "Well I'll tell you what we have planned, but firstly you have to let me tell you the whole plan before you reply, promise?" Hugh asked. "Promise" Ally replied getting worried. Hugh took a deep breath "we are going to go and stay at Ben's." Ally felt her body brace up "hang on mom, you said you'd let me finish" Hugh said, knowing very well what the look on his mom's face meant. "Then in two weeks' time Sally, John and Aden are going to come and stay for a week and we will all head up to Yellowstone together. So we are only delaying the trip by a couple of weeks. Ben said that it's fine, he's got plenty of room for everyone, and then we get to go to the BBQ and you still get to go to Yellowstone" Hugh finished, not knowing how his mom would react. Ally felt betrayed and ambushed but she didn't know why. She couldn't help but glare at Ben, "it's all his fault, he has been planting seeds of ideas in my son's mind and not taking into consideration all the consequences" she thought. Hugh saw his mom glaring at Ben and stepped in before his mom said something she regretted. "Mom it's going to be fine, I know things are changing" he said taking her hands, "but my gut feeling is this is the right thing to do, and you always wanted to spend some time on a ranch, and we get to spend it together, instead of being stuck in the pickup driving, and I think the mountain air will do you good, he has got a stream near his house that you could go and sit by. Please mom, trust me on this" he said giving her a hug. Ally took hold of Hugh and pulled him onto her knee, "is this what you really want?", "yes mom" Hugh replied sympathetically. "Someday I hope to be as sure of life as you are" Ally said bewildered.

Ally looked up at people packing things into their trucks and trailers. The fair men were busy taking down the rides and she looked back at her son. Where did he get his faith in life from? How does he know that everything will be alright? Ally looked across at Bill for encouragement, Bill smiled and nodded his head. "Ok" Ally said quietly. Hugh leapt off her lap and went over to where Aden was sitting. "Come on Aden we'll wash the pots up for my mom" and off they scurried. Ally looked at the rest of them. Sally smiled with excitement at the budding romance. John slapped his legs and stood up before his wife said something, "well that's the plan, we'll meet you at the ranch in a couple of weeks and head off to Yellowstone. Come on Sally we had better pack up the tent." Tom and Chad stood up next, "right, we'd best be making tracks." They shook Ben's hand, "see you soon Ally." Ally waved back. Bill and Helen collected the chairs and took them round the other side of the motor home.

Ally and Ben were the only ones left. Ally looked at Ben sternly – she couldn't help but feel angry and he knew it. "I hope you know what you are doing!" Ally remarked. Ben moved closer to her, "I do, Hugh had the idea and I think it's a great one, I'm not ready to say goodbye yet, I've only just found you. Please just give me two weeks to show you." "Show me what?" Ally exclaimed "share with you all the joy you make me feel whenever I'm with you, there are things going on up in the heavens, and I know that you feel them too, you can't deny it" Ben smiled. Ally looked away, she knew exactly what he meant but she certainly wasn't ready to say it aloud.

Ben took her in his arms but Ally just stayed limp. "You're safe, everything's going to be alright" he said "you won't have to lift a finger when you're at the ranch. I know you're really going to love it. I have been up all night thinking things through, and I know you have Hugh to concentrate on and look after, but that doesn't mean I can't take care of you" he whispered.

Ally's head fell onto his shoulder as she couldn't hold back the tears. They were tears of fear and of hope. Ben held her close swaying from side to side, knowing that this was a big step for her. They heard the rattle of plates. Ally pulled away from Ben and turned away from the direction Hugh and Aden were coming from. Ally quickly wiped away the tears, looking up at the sky trying to stop any more tears arriving. "I'm sorry" she said, Ben wiped away the new tears that arrived and kissed her salty cheek. "There is nothing to be sorry about" he looked into her eyes, and Ally couldn't resist the feeling of relief washing over her as she knew deep down inside that everything was going to be ok, the first time she had ever felt that since Hugh's dad was around. "Things are going to be alright aren't they?" half asking herself, half asking Ben, "yes they are" he said softly.

Ben went over to where Hugh and Aden were helping Bill and Helen to pack things away. "Right Hugh, I'll go and load up the horses and bring the truck and trailer around. If you help your mom pack up and then you can follow me back to the ranch." Hugh's eyes opened wide with excitement. He looked at Aden and they high fived. Hugh then looked at Ben and smiled, Ben smiled back ruffling Hugh's hair. Ben began to walk over to where his truck was parked.

Aden looked at Hugh "I had better get back to mom and dad", "ok" Hugh agreed. "I'll see you in two weeks' time!" They hugged and Aden ran back to his parents. Hugh came up behind Ally and gave her a big hug "thanks mom, I love you." Ally knelt down and started hugging and kissing him all over the face "I love you too, Monkey", "argh stop mom" he said laughing. "We had better get packed up before Ben gets back" Ally said. "I'm on it mom" Hugh said springing into action.

Bill and Helen put the table and the last of the chairs inside the motor home and closed the door. They made their way to the back of the truck where Ally and Hugh were busy packing. "I guess it's goodbye" Bill said holding his arms out wide. Ally walked across and hugged him back "no, just see you later" Ally kissed him on the cheek. "He's a good man that Ben, you've picked well but if he does give you any bother I'll be straight over to read him the riot act" Bill said. Ally smiled "will do." Bill moved across to Hugh "see you later, you keep on dreaming" Hugh hugged him "will do." Helen hugged Ally "you're welcome any time", "thanks, and if you ever want a place to stay in the UK our doors are always open" Ally replied. Bill and Helen made their way to the motor home and got in. The engine stirred and they pulled off, honking their horn as they went. Ally and Hugh waved until the motor home disappeared out of sight.

Just as Ally was checking around making sure they hadn't left anything, they heard a truck and trailer pull up. Hugh jumped out of their pickup and ran over. Ben wound down the window and Ally went over to join them. She couldn't help noticing how good he looked with his cap and shades on in the truck with the sound of horses munching hay in his gooseneck trailer. "Yeah, he's definitely a ranch man" she mused. Ben interrupted her thoughts, "if you guys follow me, we are heading over to a town a few hours away, it's not far." Ally laughed "your American 'not far' is my British 'hours and hundreds of miles away' to be sure." Ben smiled at her; part of him could not believe that he would have her all to himself for two full weeks.

"Ok, just make sure you don't lose us" Ally said half serious, half sarcastically. "Don't worry I'm not going to lose this precious cargo." Ally blushed. "Ok Hugh time to hit the highway" Ally cheered. Hugh ran over to the truck and turned the stereo on where "life is a highway, I wanna drive it all night long" came blaring through the speakers. Ally and Ben laughed at his enthusiasm. Ally began to walk back to the pickup "hey Miss, a kiss for the journey" Ally turned round "it's only a couple of hours." Ben took off his glasses and pulled a puppy dog look. Ally smiled and drifted towards the truck. She leaned in and gave him a kiss "I could get used to this" Ben remarked. Ally moved away smiling as she walked back to the pickup.

She climbed into the truck. Hugh had settled in with his boots off and music on as they watched Ben's truck and trailer pull off in front. Ally pressed the accelerator and off they rolled, "where the brave are free and lover's soars" Ally sang.

A few hours later they were turning into a driveway with a sign overhead made out of big tree trunks. The driveway wound through a valley, with the mountains as the back drop, forests to the left and open pasture land to the right. Hugh's head was already out of the window lapping up the view. Ally had to admit that they were right – she did love it. As they neared a large log cabin Ben stuck his arm out of the window and indicated that they should park by the house. He carried on with the truck and trailer behind some trees.

Ally parked as indicated and undid her seat belt. The house was beautiful and had such presence yet it still seemed to blend into the countryside. As she was getting out of the car Ben appeared from around the trees. Hugh got out and came round to where they were standing. "Do you want to help me unload and put the horses away?" Ben asked Hugh, "yes I'll just get my coat." As Hugh was getting his coat Ben walked up to the house and unlocked the front door. "You can take your stuff in, there's food, tea and coffee. Make yourself at home" he said to Ally. Ally reached into the truck, pulled out her handbag and made her way over to the house.

As she walked through the door she looked behind and smiled as she saw Hugh bounding along trying to keep up with Ben's long legs. As Ally stepped through the door her breath was taken away. In front of her was a large living room with an open fire, straight ahead were large patio doors framing a picture-perfect view of the land behind. To the right she saw what looked like an office and next to this, a bathroom. To her left there was a large kitchen with a sturdy oak table and cooking range. Tucked away in the corner of the living room was a staircase. Ally's gaze wandered up it and there was a balcony which looked like it led onto the bedrooms.

Ally placed her handbag down on the sofa and made her way to the kitchen. She lifted up the kettle and took it over to the sink where, out of the window, she could see a pasture full of horses. She put the kettle back and flipped the switch. Ally wondered if there was the same set-up in the kitchen as in England: cups above the kettle and spoons either left or right below the kettle. Of course it was. As the kettle hissed and then clicked as the water came to a boil, Ally placed a tea bag in the cup and filled it with hot water.

As the tea brewed Ally leant against the worktop and took in her surroundings. "Such a beautiful home", she thought, "surely he can't live here by himself?" Ally put the tea bag in the bin and poured in the milk. She made her way out of the front door and went in the direction the boys had gone. As she moved past the row of trees it opened up to a large American barn. She saw Hugh pulling a trolley twice the size of him full of hay to one of the stables. As she entered the barn she saw Ben taking the tack from the trailer and putting it in what looked like a tack room.

The smell of hay and horses filled the air. "I'm home" Ally thought. "Nearly done" Hugh shouted from one of the stables. Ally meandered down the centre of the barn looking at the horses that had just been taken off the trailer, eagerly tucking into their hay. Ben came out of the tack room and closed the door. He walked up the aisle to where Ally stood, "find everything alright?" he asked, "yes thanks" Ally said holding up a mug of tea. "All done Ben" Hugh said breathlessly, "thanks mate that was a great help" Ben replied looking around the barn, checking the horses one last time.

"Shall we head back to the house and get ready for the BBQ?" Ben said as Ally was reaching out and stroked a horse's head and its velvet nose. "That one is showing signs of being a great star" Ben stated proudly. Ally looked into the mare's eyes and all she saw was unconditional love, a kind of love you can only get from animals.

The three of them walked out of the barn and back to the house. "Right, I had better show you to your rooms" Ben said. Ally and Hugh stopped at the car to get their suitcases. Ben took hold of Ally's and brought it in the house as Hugh pulled his mini case along on wheels.

They headed across the living room to the staircase. As they reached the top they went along the internal balcony which overlooked the living room. Ben pointed to a small room with a single bed in "this one's for you Hugh." Hugh went in, dived straight onto the bed and put his hands behind his head "yep this'll do quite nicely" he replied. Ben chuckled and he walked with Ally to the next room which had a double bed, en suite bathroom and a window looking out onto the mountains. "This one is for you" he said looking into her eyes, "thank you" Ally replied taking her suitcase and putting it next to the bed. They went back onto the balcony "and if you get scared at night" Ben said looking at Ally "my room's just here" he headed to a room at the end of the balcony. Ally couldn't resist being nosey as she peered round the door. It had a hand carved wooden king sized bed, a small sofa, dresser and large sliding doors that led onto a balcony. On the balcony was a small table with matching chairs overlooking an incredible view of large open grassland and a small river.

Ally was definitely impressed and her mind wandered into a daydream. She thought of waking up in the morning, sliding open the doors and having a cup of tea whilst watching the sun rise. "Just in case you get scared at night and need a hug" Ben said cheekily with his eyes twinkling. "Right, I'm going to get showered and then I'll crank up the BBQ before everyone starts to arrive" Ben stated. Ally got the hint and moved out of the doorway back to her room where she opened her suitcase and began to unpack.

Hugh popped his head round the door, "hey you" Ally said as she was hanging up one of her skirts. She saw Hugh march through her room with a towel round his waist and wash bag under his arms into the en suite. "When did her little boy get so grown up?" Ally thought. As she heard Hugh singing in the shower she slipped into the bed and thought she'd have a quick snooze. "I'll just have five minutes' sleep while Hugh is in the shower" she thought as she closed her eyes and drifted off to sleep.

Ben stuck his head through Ally's door as he was making his way downstairs. He saw Ally looking so peaceful as she slept. Hugh came out of the shower and stood next to him. He looked up at Ben "it's the first time I have seen her properly sleep, normally she is so restless." Ben looked back at Ally, pleased that she had started to lower her barriers; no longer does he have to get past the flaming archers to enter the castle that surrounds her heart.

"Shall we start getting things ready for the BBQ?" Ben asked Hugh. They made their way downstairs where Ben opened up the patio doors and headed over to the BBQ to light it.

Ally turned over and heard laughter and talking. She opened her sleepy eyes and reached for her phone – it dawned on her that she had been asleep for five hours! But the bed continued to invite her back into the land of dreams but then she heard Hugh's voice from downstairs and she shuffled in the bed to a more upright position to try to wake up.

"The BBQ must have started" Ally thought, rubbing her eyes sleepily whilst pulling back the duvet. She made her way to the bathroom to wash off the smell of the country fair and rodeo. As Ally was finishing getting dressed and began to brush her hair she heard footsteps coming up the stairs. She saw Ben in the reflection of the mirror holding a cup of tea. "How did you sleep?" he enquired, "like a log" Ally replied "it's a very comfy bed, maybe too comfy." Ben smiled, gently running his fingertips through her hair. "There's food downstairs when you're ready" Ben said as he made his way out of the room.

Ally was finished getting ready but was putting off going downstairs to meet everyone. That definitely wasn't one of her strengths. She normally she has Hugh there who knows everyone within the first five minutes of arriving. "I can't put it off any longer" Ally said to herself in the mirror, and she headed out of the room and down the stairs. She walked across the living room to the kitchen, glancing out of the patio doors where she saw people eating and laughing, and kids playing. Ally placed her mug next to the sink when Hugh came whizzing in "excuse me mom" I need to get another plate, Ally moved out the way of the cupboard door.

Hugh pulled out a plate "is everything ok?" Ally asked. "Yes, I am Ben's chief" Hugh replied. Ally nodded and followed Hugh out of the kitchen and across the living room. As she walked through the patio doors she saw Ben at the BBQ flipping over some steaks. He looked up and smiled at her, grabbed a plate and put a steak on it. He came across to her and pointed to a table where there was salad, rice and much more besides. "Thanks" Ally said, taking the plate and making her way over to where the rest of the food was. Ben headed back to his BBQ where he was putting on more meat.

After filling up her plate Ally found an empty seat and tucked in. The sleep had definitely worked up an appetite. A lady came to sit next to her "hi I'm Lilly", "hi" Ally motioned with her hands as she had a mouthful of food. Ally finished her mouthful and looked over at Lilly "how are you?" Ally asked, "good thanks" Lilly replied. "You must be Ally?" Ally looked surprised and Lilly gestured over to where Hugh was. "Don't worry, Hugh has been telling us all how you both met Ben", "oh" Ally nodded taking another mouthful of food.

Ally should have known that the whole town would know their story by now. There's no stopping that child and his dreams. Ally finished her meal and put the plate on the ground. Ben came across to sit down next to her with a plate full of food. Ally looked at him "have you finished your chief duties?" Ben motioned over to the BBQ where there was another man supervising the grills as he took a bite out of his burger. Ben turned to Lilly "how did you get on at the fair?", "good thanks, we sold quite a lot of gear, it was a good turnout" Lilly said, happy with how the past four days had gone. Ben nodded in agreement, Ally looked at Lilly curiously "what do you sell?" But before Lilly could answer Ben jumped in "the best tack around" Lilly smiled at the complement. Ben looked at Ally "do you want any more?" pointing at her empty plate. "No I'm alright thanks, I am just going to digest this plate first, maybe later." With that he was off back to the grill.

As the night wore on everyone settled in a circle around a fire and there was someone strumming a guitar in the background. Ben had pulled a chair up next to Ally's. Hugh was busy playing with the dog. Ally suddenly realised what time it was, she got up and headed over to Hugh "come on you it's time for bed", "oh mom, please, five more minutes" Hugh groaned. "No come on, you had a late night last night as well" Ally stated "can Patches come with me?" Hugh asked pointing to the dog that was sitting obediently by his side. "No I don't think the dog is allowed in the house", "mom you don't know that" Hugh said stubbornly. Ally turned to Ben "are dogs allowed in the house and upstairs? Hugh wants Patches to sleep in his room tonight." Ben looked up "yes sure, just no dogs allowed on the beds", "see I told you mom" Hugh said. "Hey, less of the attitude and upstairs to bed" Ally said sternly.

The trip and all the changes had really started to wear on Ally's emotions and she felt drained like she was going through a life detox. Hugh made his way through the patio doors with Patches by his side. As Ally sat back down and took a gulp of wine she heard Hugh from the bathroom telling Patches that he needed to clean his teeth before going to bed. She couldn't stay mad at him for long. Hugh appeared at the patio doors in his pyjamas and went round everyone giving them a hug and kiss, saying goodnight, knowing everyone by name.

When he reached Ben he climbed up on Ben's knees and gave him a big bear hug "night Ben, thank you for everything". "Night night Hugh, thank you for being a star today." Ally looked up at the night sky trying to hold back the tears. Hugh climbed down and took hold of Ally's hand and off they went upstairs. Ben watched as they walked into the house. "Now it's a home" he thought.

Ally sat back in her chair. Ben took up his usual position draping his arm casually around the back of her chair. Ally reached down for her glass and noticed it felt heavier. She looked at Ben "have the refill fairies been again?" He chuckled "nothing to do with me." Ally settled into the conversations around her, sharing the news of the trip and journey so far. As she told the story it no longer felt like a reminder of a tragedy but an adventure with its highs and lows. For the first time for a long time she felt relaxed and comfortable, and most of all she felt at home.

The last of the guest drifted off as Ben said goodbye to them. Ally collected the last of the remaining glasses and took them through to the kitchen. Ben came in behind her, twirled her around and they started to dance around the kitchen. Ally melted in his arms, Ben spun her round and lifted her into his arms, and they embraced with a long kiss. As their lips parted they both smiled, looking into each other's eyes "I've been waiting all night to do that" Ben said lovingly.

Ben put Ally down and she picked up her glass of water. "Night night" Ally said, "night" Ben replied. Ally headed upstairs as Ben followed her turning off the lights. Ally turned into her room. As Ben walked by he had one final look at the incredible woman stood before him and headed to his room. Ally watched as he walked into his room and then slowly closed her door as waves of happiness flowed around her body.

8 DREAMS BECOMING REALITY

Hugh, with Patches, slowly opened the bedroom door. The sun was just rising in the sky and Hugh tried to stop the door creaking so as not to wake his mom and Ben. Patches waited patiently behind him, poised ready for the ok. When the gap was large enough to slip through Hugh made his way out onto the balcony then crept downstairs. Patches headed straight for the patio doors and looked round to Hugh "do you want to go out Patches?" Hugh asked as he opened the door. Patches went out through the door and was off to do her morning check around the ranch to make sure everything was in order and how she had left it the night before.

Hugh left the door open so Patches could make her way back in when she was done. As he walked across the living room he ran his hands along the back of the couch and looked at the log fire. He dreamed of his mom sitting in front of the fire creating her future, Ben and him watching a movie on the TV being a family once again. He smiled to himself "right, let's get this masterpiece rolling, there's no point in having a dream if I don't take some action to help it come true" he thought to himself.

He went into the kitchen and put the kettle on. As he was making a cup of tea he checked what was in the fridge: eggs, bacon, mushrooms and sausages. He closed the fridge door, lifted up the bread bin lid and saw a loaf. "Cooked breakfast it is then" he mumbled to himself. He took his cup of tea and sat at the kitchen table. As he looked out of the kitchen window and had a sip of tea, "what is it that I now want to come true?" he said to himself. "What is it that I really want, if I had one wish what would I want it to be?" Hugh took out his phone and scrolled through the pictures he had taken of his vision wall before he left.

When he reached the part of the wall which had the pictures of America he paused to look at them. There was a picture of the flag, of a country fair and rodeo, a young boy roping, him and his mom hugging and then a picture of him riding a horse with a herd of cattle. There was one dream left to come true, yet they had many weeks left in America. "My dream wasn't big enough" Hugh thought, "I need to add some more to it." He fetched his diary and sat back at the table:

Dear Dan the Diary,

I have nearly completed all the things I wished to do on our trip in America, so I want to add some more: to ride Firefly and help Ben with the cattle, to be a roping champion, to go to Yellowstone with mom, Ben, John, Sally and Aden, to stay in a log cabin, to go fishing and to go on yet more adventures. I also want to be a family again like it was when dad was alive – with mom, Ben and me. I think that's about it except one final thing if wishes do come true. I wish to have another dad. Mom has been doing a great job but having a dad means I can do man things with him the things mom just doesn't get.

Hugh

Hugh closed the diary and looked back out of the window, "if you don't ask then you don't get, I know these things will come true as well, with perfect timing." He felt a dog's head on his lap, Patches had returned from her rounds, "shall we get started?" he smiled cheekily at Patches. Patches barked in response and sat down by Hugh's side awaiting the next order. Hugh got up from his chair and made his way to the kitchen to start cooking breakfast. Patches was glued to his side, ready to hoover up any pieces of food that fell on the floor.

Ben made his way downstairs, humming a song to himself. As he approached the kitchen he saw the kitchen table all set out with plates, a jug of orange juice and the bread cut into slices with the butter placed next to it. He then looked across to see Hugh standing at the stove watching the contents in the frying pan. "Morning" Ben smiled, putting the coffee machine on "morning Ben, is mom up yet? Breakfast's nearly ready." Ben glanced up at the balcony, "I think she's still asleep." Hugh frowned and made his way into the living room "mom, mom, mom quick" he screamed urgently. Ally came darting out of her room and looked over the balcony and down into the living room where Hugh was standing.

"What's wrong?" she said, breathless as the adrenaline was flowing with vengeance around her body. "Breakfast is ready" Hugh smiled sweetly. Ally looked at him "you could have just come up to tell me instead of yelping and frightening me" Ally said angrily and disappeared into her room. Hugh headed back to the kitchen where Ben was drinking his coffee. Hugh looked at him "you had better go and tame the wild mustang" he said before going back to his cooking. Ben smiled, made a cup of tea and headed upstairs. As he approached Ally's room he heard her muttering to herself, he tapped lightly on the door and pushed it open.

Ally spun round quickly, ready to give Hugh a piece of her mind. She stopped suddenly "oh, it's you" she said and carried on getting ready. Ben walked across the room and put down the cup of tea. He made his way across to Ally and took her in his arms "morning Miss Ally" he said, kissing her on the cheeks then moving to her lips. Ally's arms slid around his waist as she said "morning Mr" between kisses. Ben began to melt away every bad feeling and thought she had experienced so far that morning.

"It's a beautiful day, I'm in the company of a beautiful girl and we have had our breakfast cooked for us by a wonderful boy, what a perfect day!" Ben exclaimed looking into Ally's eyes. He scooped her up, causing Ally to giggle, and carried her to the kitchen where Hugh was just finishing serving up the breakfast. "I caught me a wild one" Ben exclaimed putting Ally down, "good look taming that one" Hugh said sarcastically. "Hey you, less of the cheek" Ally said sitting at the table. "Wow, Hugh, you have definitely outdone yourself this time, thank you Monkey" Ally said, proud of her son. "Tuck in before it gets cold then" Hugh said, putting a piece of bacon on the floor for Patches, and joining Ally and Ben at the table.

Ben leant back in his chair to let his food digest as Ally began to collect the empty plates and load up the dishwasher. "What are your plans today?" Ally asked

Hugh and Ben. Hugh looked at Ben, hoping his response was to go and work the cattle. "Well I've got to go and do some fencing today up on the hill ready to move the cattle into the new pasture at the end of the week" he looked at Hugh "do you wanna come?" Hugh looked out the window disappointed – it wasn't quite what he had in mind but it might be fun he thought.

"Sure" Hugh said, leaving the table and making his way upstairs to clean his teeth. Ally looked at Ben with a sympathetic smile. "My dad used to say to me 'you can't just do the fun jobs all the time because in no time at all they won't be fun anymore', it made me realise that by getting the not-so-fun jobs done first it makes the fun jobs even better" Ben said looking at Ally. "It sounds like your dad is a wise man, it wouldn't do Hugh any harm to get his hands dirty and learn a few skills, I'm afraid life hasn't been much fun for him back in the UK. l have been too wrapped up in my own thoughts" Ally said, leaning against the worktop. "It's definitely time for things to change, for me to change, Hugh deserves better and so do I" Ally said, deep in thought.

Ben got up and walked across to Ally "you were doing the best you could right then, and now we can do the best we can together, anyway it would be nice to spend some time with Hugh and have a chance to get to know each other better." "I bet you didn't really count on having to nurture two relationships" Ally remarked. Ben beamed "hmm so this is a relationship is it?" Ally's face turned to shock "no I mean…oh you know what I mean, go on and have your man time" Ally said, trying to brush over her remark. Ben leaned across and kissed her, "I can't think of any better way to spend my time than in nurturing our relationship."

Hugh arrived back wearing his coat and boots "ready" he said. Ben moved away from Ally "well, we'll load up the truck and head up the hill for some man time." Hugh looked up at Ben, his frown turned into a smile "bye mom, me and Ben are off to do the fencing, come on Patches" he strolled outside. Ally smiled at her little legend, "see you later" Ben said tipping his hat, as he disappeared outside following Hugh.

"So do you know how to drive?" Ben asked, getting into the truck. "No, silly, I'm too young and my feet don't reach the pedals" Hugh laughed. "Well how about you steer and I do the pedals?" Ben compromised as he remembered when he was young how his dad had done the same. "Alright then" Hugh said climbing onto Ben's lap. As the truck began to roll forward Hugh began to turn the steering wheel towards the gate that led to the pasture. As they reached the gate Ally came up to the side of the truck. She looked into the cab and saw Hugh behind the wheel, "hey monkey" she pointed. "Floor it Ben before mom stops us!" Hugh shouted with excitement. Ben revved the engine and they went through the gate at top speed waving at Ally.

As they reached the top of the hill Hugh noticed the fence wire was broken and wooden posts were lying on the ground. "We'll park the truck just on that flat area up there" Ben said, pointing ahead of them. Hugh steered the truck and as they reached the spot Ben put it into park and turned off the engine. He opened the door and Hugh jumped out first with Ben following. They made their way round to the back of the truck and pulled out a tool bag. Hugh got a reel of wire and a sledge hammer out and they made their way over to where the fence was broken.

Hugh began to stand the fence posts up in their proper position. Ben picked up the sledge hammer, "stand back Hugh", as Ben took hold of the post and began to knock it back into the ground. Hugh moved across to the next post and they worked their way along the fence line. As Ben was knocking in the last of the posts Hugh went to get the new wire. Together they put new strands of wire across as the sun moved across the sky.

Ben finished putting the last bit of wire up, "good job" Hugh said high fiving Ben. "Thanks for your help little man, I would have been up here all day doing this if I had to do it on my own" Ben replied.

They loaded the tools into the back of the pickup. As Hugh was climbing into the driver's seat, Ben called out "hang on, there is something I want to show you." He motioned for Hugh to follow him. Hugh closed the truck door and followed Ben up the hill with Patches by his side.

Ben stopped and waited for Hugh to catch with him. Hugh followed Ben's gaze and there in front of them was a valley that went all the way to the horizon, scattered with small forests, green grass and a small river running through the bottom. As the sun shone on the land, it gleamed with life and the river sparkled. Ben sat down, Hugh was mesmerized by the incredible view – he had never seen anything so perfect, everything co-existing in harmony with each other.

As the minutes went by, the silence was filled with gratitude of what was in front of them. Hugh took a deep breath, breathing in all the life around him, letting the fresh air fill every inch of his lungs. He then let out a sigh as every memory of the times when life had pushed him to his limits and he thought he couldn't go on anymore left his body and melted into the ground. This was replaced with a peace that tingled around his body.

He sat down next to Ben. "This is incredible, I feel incredible" he said, looking happily at Ben. Ben smiled at Hugh, feeling the same warmth and life from the surroundings. Hugh moved across and leant against Ben. "I come up here every week" Ben began, "and sit dreaming about different things. This is where I saw myself winning the championships, where I have run through business deals and conversations I had yet to have, and a love I was yet to experience." Hugh looked up at Ben. "Did you know you were going to meet me and mom?", "I had an inkling, see down there" Ben pointed to a small wood near the river's edge "the day before I set off for the fair I came up here and a deer and her young fawn made their way down to the river for a drink. A few minutes later a stag joined them and drank next to them. They then all made their way into woods and as I watched them my body filled with a feeling of happiness and love, nothing like I had ever felt before. My grandad used to tell me stories of nature's omens, clues Mother Nature gives us that what we have wished for is coming true" Ben continued. Hugh listened intently, "and then when I met you and Bill I knew that you were that young fawn. When I saw your mom dancing for the first time I got a flashback of the scene of the deer and stag drinking together by the water's edge."

Hugh didn't know which question to start with. "So are you telling me that life leaves clues? And how do you know if it is a clue? And, and…" Hugh couldn't get any more words out of his mouth as his mind was trying to comprehend what he had just heard. Ben smiled "yes, life leaves clues. When you make a wish or have a desire, and if you spot something that seems to stand out, or relates to that wish or desire, then you know that life is doing what it can to make it come true, and you know it's true because of that gut feeling you have. My grandad brought me to this very spot and this is where I found out about nature's omens. I am so grateful for you circling my ranch on your map and coming here, so I could pass this knowledge on to you" Ben finished, looking back over the valley.

Hugh didn't know what to say as he let one of life's secrets filter into his heart "Ben, I know me and mom are only here for a few weeks, and I know this may be a big ask, but just while we are here, would you be my dad? Because I know my real dad brought you to us and you are just as much of a dad to me as he was but in cowboy boots and a cowboy hat instead." Ben's eyes sparkled as his eyes filled up with tears of happiness, "I would be honoured" he said as he hugged Hugh.

Hugh was sitting leaning against Ben's chest as they sat in silence looking out over the valley. "Ben, can we make a wish together and see if life leaves any clues?" Hugh asked, breaking the silence. "What do you have in mind?" Ben asked looking at Hugh. "That me and mom stay where our new home is and begin a new life together as a new family" Hugh looked up at Ben. "Would you like your new home to be here with me at the ranch?" Ben asked. Hugh's eyes sparkled with excitement "yes, this is home", "well then, we shall have to wait and see if the clues present themselves" Ben said. He looked up at the sky as dusk was beginning to descend.

"We had better head back to your mom as she will be wondering where we are" Ben said. Hugh got up and Ben followed him. Hugh reached across and took hold of Ben's hand "thank you for showing me the valley, and sharing with me the things your grandad shared with you." "Oh there's lots more of that, my grandad had lots of stories, thank you for following your gut feelings and bringing us all together" Ben said as they reached the truck. Ben got in first and Hugh climbed into position behind the steering wheel.

As the truck made its way down the hill, Hugh moved the steering wheel left and right to dodge the rocks. Ben slowed the truck down as they reached the gate. As they got closer, they saw a robin sitting on the gate. Hugh's head spun round "do you see the robin?" he exclaimed. Ben brought the truck to a halt in front of the gate as they both watched the robin fly off. "Was that one of nature's clues?" Hugh asked. Ben's eyes followed the robin as it took flight "well they say that robins are the sign of new beginnings." He then looked straight ahead as he saw Ally making her way across to open the gate. Ben and Hugh looked at each other and smiled gleefully. "Can we keep this between us?" Hugh asked "what happens with the lads stays with the lads?" Ben smiled as the truck began to roll forward through the gate.

They parked the truck and Hugh got out, closely followed by Ben. "So how was your day?" Ally asked. "It was alright" Hugh said "we got the fencing done." He shrugged and made his way into the house, trying hard to hide his excitement. Ally turned to Ben "is everything alright?" she asked, "it's perfect, Hugh was a great help" Ben replied. They made their way into the house. As Ben walked through the front door the smell of food filled his nostrils "something smells good" he said. Ally smiled shyly and walked across to the kitchen, "I thought you guys might be hungry when you got back so I have made a shepherd's pie" as she peered into the oven.

Hugh walked up to the kitchen sink, rolling back his sleeves. "When's dinner mom?" he said washing his hands. "Whenever you guys are ready" Ally replied, picking up her cup of tea. Ben leaned against the door frame, taking in the picture before him, as he saw his dreams begin to come true. He moved towards the table and took a seat "well I'm ready" he said, "me too" Hugh said, sitting next to him. "Well that settles that" Ally said, placing the shepherd's pie in the middle of the table.

When they had finished their meal Hugh began to stack the dishwasher whilst Ally wiped the table. Ben had gone into his office to do some paperwork. Ally put the dishcloth by the sink. "How about we light the log fire and have a movie night?" Ally asked Hugh. "That's a great idea mom, I will get things ready for the movie if you sort out the fire." Hugh closed the dishwasher door and disappeared into the living room across to where a large cabinet stood. On the bottom shelf there was row after row of DVDs; he scanned across the titles for one he liked the look of.

Ally made her way across to the office and stuck her head around the door. "Do you mind if I light the fire tonight? We thought it would be nice to have a movie night" Ally said. Ben looked up from his computer screen at Ally, "yeah no problem, the wood's just round the back and there is a box of matches on the fireplace, do you know what to do?" Ally's face turned to disgust "we have log fires back in England too so I think I'll manage" she replied sarcastically, and disappeared out of sight. Ben shook his head, that wasn't what he meant; he went back to filling in the information on the database.

Hugh had a bag of popcorn and was emptying its contents into a bowl. He then opened a bag of crisps and emptied them into a separate bowl. He carried them through to the living room where Ally was busy arranging newspapers and little sticks in the fireplace. She lit the newspaper and the fire came to life, she added a bit more wood then turned round and surveyed the room. "I'll close the curtains" she said getting up, "I'll get the duvet" Hugh said running across the living room and up the stairs. "Timber!" he shouted as he threw the duvet over the edge of the balcony where it landed on the living room floor.

He came back downstairs and put the DVD in the DVD player before climbing under the duvet that Ally had spread over the couch. Ally added more wood to the fire before joining Hugh. "Come on Ben we're ready" Hugh shouted before putting a large handful of popcorn in his mouth. "I'll just go and get something" Ally said, sliding out from under the duvet. Making her way across to where her handbag was she pulled out her diary and some pictures she had printed off the computer earlier on that day.

As she reached the couch, Hugh began "how is your diary going mom?" "It's going alright, I am definitely writing a different story to the one I was writing a few weeks ago. I have printed the photo of all of us when we were at the bar." She showed him the picture of Bill, Helen, Chad, Tom, Ben, Sally, Aden, John, Hugh and Ally all sitting round a table. Ally opened the diary up to today's date and added the picture.

Dear Diary,

Above is a photo of all those who have helped change the course my path has taken. They have filled my life with happiness and love. These are the people I have met on our adventure so far – it was taken at the country fair and rodeo bar. For the dreams I have yet to experience, well, they will be set out below. Hugh has reminded me of how magical life is and he has helped to re-awaken my love for life. It's maybe a little bit smaller than Hugh's vision wall but these are the dreams I want to experience

Love always

Ally

Ally began to stick in the other pictures she had printed off the computer. Writing little notes by the side of them Hugh watched over her shoulder as she began to create her new future, full of desires. As Ally stuck in the last picture and viewed her masterpiece she smiled "that's an awesome future mom" Hugh said proudly. "I love you so much" Hugh said, flinging his arms around her neck and kissing her. "I couldn't have done it without you, never stop believing in life and most of all yourself" Ally whispered to him.

At that moment Ben walked into the living room "is there space for one more?" "Yeah you can go here next to me" Hugh pointed to a free space on the couch. Ben sat down pulling the duvet over his legs, "well this is a first for me" he said taking a handful of crisps. "Me and mom always used to have movie nights, they're the best" Hugh said, pressing the play button. Ben stretched his arm out along the back of the couch and began to gently stroke Ally's hair. Ally looked across and in the darkness she could see his eyes sparkle with affection. She turned her head and kissed his hand, and then the intro music of the movie began.

Hugh was up early again. The last couple of days had been spent getting everything ready to move the cattle. Ben had arranged for some friends from a local ranch to come over and help for the day. Hugh couldn't sit still, he was dashing around making breakfast for everyone and clearing up the pots as soon as they had finished their last mouthful. He wanted to get out to the horses as soon as possible. Ben watched Hugh as he buzzed around; working with the cattle was also one of his favourite things to do and he was secretly just as excited.

"All done" Hugh shouted. "I'll go and get my coat and boots on" he said, just about to disappear from the kitchen. "Hang on there Monkey, just take a seat for a minute, there are a few things to discuss." Hugh's face dropped. "Can't we talk about it later?" Hugh pleaded. He wasn't interested in having delays or chats, not today. "No Hugh, it's important" Ally said more sternly to emphasise the fact that this wasn't open for negotiation. Hugh shuffled his feet across the floor and sat back down at the table. He looked at his mom "when you're out there, make sure you do exactly as Ben tells you" Ally began "yes mom, of course I will" Hugh said frustrated. "Wait there, I just need to get something" Ally said getting up from the table. Hugh looked across at Ben in desperation but Ben just smiled and gave him a wink. Hugh looked back in the direction Ally had gone.

Ally reappeared holding a bag "right, if you're going to help out, you'll need a few things." Hugh looked at her confused. Ally pulled out a small pair of cowboy boots "you can't ride for hours in your other boots, so you'll need these." Hugh was shocked and gingerly took the cowboy boots in his hands, running his fingers over the patterned stitching. Ally then reached in and pulled out a belt which had a buckle with a horse on it, "and you'll need a belt until you receive your own championship roping buckle." Hugh was speechless as Ally laid the belt on the table. "Here are some gloves too, and last but not least, you'll be needing a ranch rope." Hugh shot out of his chair and flew into Ally's arms "thank you, thank you, thank you" he said giving her lots of kisses.

"It wasn't just me, you'll have to thank someone else too" she said, looking in the direction of Ben. Hugh made his way round the table and Ben pulled him up onto his knees. Hugh wrapped his arms around Ben's neck, "thanks dad" he whispered "any time son" Ben replied pulling him in closer. Hugh climbed down and walked over to where his gifts were lying on the table. He took hold of the belt and threaded it through the top of his jeans and then pulled on his cowboy boots. Ben disappeared to get his boots and hat on. Hugh then got the gloves and put one in each pocket of his coat. Finally he took hold of the rope and stepped back so that Ally could survey her young man ready for the ranch. Ben returned to the kitchen, "ready!" Hugh said eagerly. Ben brought a hat round from behind his back and placed it on Hugh's head, "now you're ready for the ranch." Hugh beamed and gave Ally and Ben another hug. "Right, can you go and tack her up?" Ben asked looking at Hugh. "Seriously?" Hugh said in disbelief, "yes if you're quick" Ben smiled. Hugh ran out of the front door and across to the barn.

Ally got up from the table and walked across to Ben, taking him in her arms. "Thank you for everything" she said. Ben leaned in and kissed her "have a great day Miss Ally." Ally chuckled "how could today be anything less than perfect – I've got you haven't I?" Ben gave her one last kiss and headed outside.

As he reached the barn Hugh was already carrying Firefly's tack over to her stall. Ben followed him and as Hugh was putting on her bridle, Ben lifted on her saddle and cinched it up. Ben then walked to the tack room to get his horse's tack. On his return he heard Hugh talking to Firefly, telling her about the new things he had been given, how he couldn't wait to spend all day with her and about fixing the fence. Firefly stood still listening to his every word. Ben smiled and began tacking up his horse, "is she ready Hugh?" Ben enquired. "Yes" Hugh replied, peering over the stall door, "well bring her out and you can get on over by those bales of hay" Ben suggested.

Hugh pushed the stall door open and made his way across the barn aisle to where a stack of hay bales were. Firefly followed his footsteps and Hugh climbed up onto the bales so he was level with the saddle. Firefly knew the routine and positioned herself next to the bales so Hugh could get on. "Thanks girl" Hugh said, rubbing her neck before putting his foot in the stirrup and swinging his leg over.

Ben came across with Hugh's new rope and tied it to the saddle. He ran his hand down Firefly's cinch to check it was tight enough "you're good to go" said Ben. Ben moved across to where his horse was standing and put his toe in the stirrup. With one movement he swung up into the saddle. "Shall we make tracks?" Ben asked, moving his horse forward towards Firefly. "Ready!" Hugh replied, ecstatic. They made their way out of the barn, over to where the group of cowboys were waiting.

Ally made her way to the gate and swung it open. She leant on it as she held it open. The horses and cowboys began to make their way through and head up the track. Hugh and Ben were the last to ride through the gate. As Hugh rode past he tipped his hat to Ally, she smiled and nodded her head in acknowledgement. Ben came through last and leant down giving Ally a kiss, "see you later" Ally replied, closing the gate. As she watched Ben and Hugh ride up the track with Patches following on behind, she leant on the gate. The sun was just starting to rise in the sky bringing a new day full of new opportunities. Her smile grew as she watched the two of them ride off towards the horizon. "Follow your heart's desires, fulfil your dreams and allow for love to transform" Ally thought to herself.

9 EPILOGUE

As Ally walked back into the house she looked out of
the patio windows and saw the stream glistening in
the sunlight. Ally grabbed her coat and opened the
patio door. She made her way down to the stream,
allowing the fresh air to fill her body with life.

As Ally reached the water's edge she found a spot to
sit for a while and watch nature buzz around her. She
looked down to see her reflection in the water. As she
looked, a thought floated across her mind:

"Life is magical with its twists and turns, sometimes
not knowing that happiness is awaiting us just around
the next corner. If only we had the courage to seek
and keep moving forward, as we watch the love that
fills our life transform around us as we go."

ABOUT THE AUTHOR

Naomi Sharp trained as an Occupational Therapist but became fascinated with how horses help people to heal, not only physically but also mentally and emotionally. Her passion for understanding how we can help our bodies to heal and our dreams to become reality has brought some breath-taking experiences into her life as well as giving her the opportunity to meet some incredible people and visit some inspiring places.

www.spiritofthephoenix.co.uk

Printed in Great Britain
by Amazon.co.uk, Ltd.,
Marston Gate.